BISHOP'S SNOWY LEAP BOOK 1

KATHI S. BARTON

This is a work of fiction. Names, characters, places, and incidents are products of the author's imagination or are used fictitiously and are not to be construed as real. Any resemblance to actual events, locations, organizations, or persons, living or dead, is entirely coincidental.

World Castle Publishing, LLC
Pensacola, Florida
Copyright © Kathi S. Barton 2019
Paperback ISBN: 9781950890248
eBook ISBN: 9781950890255
First Edition World Castle Publishing, LLC, June 20, 2019
http://www.worldcastlepublishing.com
Licensing Notes
Cover: Karen Fuller
Editor: Maxine Bringenberg

Chapter 1

"Bishop, you have a phone call on line one." Sawyer lifted the phone up to connect when the guy at the other desk told him that he thought it was his mom. "She doesn't sound upset either."

That really was a relief. His mom had been caring for his dad for the past two weeks. Dad had taken a nasty fall, and had been found in the creek not far from their home. He was going to be okay, but he was very weak from getting a bad cold, something unusual but not unheard of for a tiger. Shifting didn't fix a cold, unfortunately.

"Mom, everything all right?" She laughed. "Well, that's a good sign. How's Dad? You know that I'll be home this weekend, right?"

"Yes, I wanted to tell you that your dad is feeling much better. Today he came into the kitchen and asked for a big breakfast. You know what that is, remember?" He did. Biscuits and gravy, fried eggs, bacon, and fresh sliced tomatoes. "He ate every bite of it too. Right now he's sitting out on the swing enjoying the afternoon sun."

"I'm so glad to hear that, Mom. Tell him not to overdo it. I'll be down this weekend like I said to do the mowing and trimming. I think the rest of them are coming home too, right?" She said that she was fixing a large meal for them all. "That'll be wonderful. I'm sick of fast food and things from the microwave."

"You'll be all right once you move home. Have you given your notice yet? I don't want to push you, son, but we sure could use you around here at times. Just having you here is a balm to my heart." He said that he'd given it yesterday. "Good. No pressure, you know, but I'm so happy that you'll be coming back home. Not that you're far away, but it's nice to know that you'll only be a phone call and a short ride from home."

After hanging up, Sawyer looked over the case notes that he'd taken. Yesterday, if nothing else, had made him want to be at home. He'd been on a domestic call, and the woman had shot her husband four times in the chest before turning the gun on herself. It had happened so quickly that he'd had no time to react. His partner had been shot too, when one of the bullets she fired first had gone astray and hit him.

"You heard from Carl yet?" He shook his head at one of the cops in the squad room with him. "I still think he shot himself so that he could be home with the kids these first few weeks of summer vacation. If it had been me, I'd have been right here at work regardless of the wound in my leg. I love my kids, but hell, they can be worse than a call out in the middle of lunch if you ask me."

No one that he worked with, it seemed, liked their families. Well, they certainly didn't want to be around them very long. One guy he worked with sent his kids to summer camp every year so that his wife could have some peace and quiet, even though he couldn't afford it.

Sawyer had his parents and his brothers. That was all he ever wanted in family. He'd seen too many households ripped apart in his line of work, and there was no way that he was going to have that kind of upset in his life. It was bad enough that he had to work with this crazy shit; there wasn't any way that he was going to go home to it as well.

He wasn't totally against marriage and children. Sawyer was just around too much domestic crap to think that every marriage was like his parents'. They had loved each other forever, it seemed to him. And they were kind to each other. Sure they argued, but not with guns or fists.

At lunch he went to his favorite place and had his usual meal. He might miss this, people who seemed to know him when he came in, brought him his favorite drink of tea, and then set his lunch in front of him. He wondered if they had it ready before he got there, the service was so fast. But he didn't care. It was hot, good, and cheap.

He didn't make much money as a cop. Sawyer used to think that was all right—he really loved his job. But lately, just over the last few months, he'd felt as if he could do better. That there was a job out there that would fulfill him in more ways than he could imagine. Finding it might be the issue, he thought. Sometime he'd have to start looking if he wanted to find it. Smiling, he dug into his lunch.

Walking back to the station house, he was glad that he was going to be spending his last two weeks on desk duty. He'd never realized it, but when someone gave their notice here, they had to work on the desk. The department apparently didn't want you killed in action just before you left. Christ, any way to save a buck or two was all anyone ever thought about.

His desk was just the way he'd left it, messy with the reports that he'd been going over. He was the speller in the group of men and women, and they would often give him their reports so that he could find the misspelled words. Usually there weren't that many, but Carl, his partner, had the worst kind of spelling ability. Like none.

Carl was forever spelling *aloud* for *allowed*. Sawyer didn't have any idea why he couldn't get that one word right. Not that there weren't a lot more that he'd misspell. Like *thanks* was *tanks*. *Friends* was forever *fiends*. Sawyer was glad that Carl would be out for a month—he'd not miss his work.

At five he made his way home. It was just a small place, but he'd lived there for the last six years. Sawyer had spent a lot of time in his little home, and had made it look as homey as he could. His mom had crocheted him a blanket for the back of his couch, and he had pictures of all his family—five brothers and his parents—in frames all over the place.

Sitting on the couch to relax before microwaving him something to eat, he closed his eyes for just a moment. The knock at the door startled him awake, and he went to see who it was. Not fully awake, he had to stare at Gunner a great deal before he knew who he was. His brother had lost some weight, it looked like, and he had on his greens.

"You look as bad as I feel." Telling his brother that he was sorry, he invited him in. When Gunner walked by him to go the couch, he smelled the fresh blood. "Are you all right? Why are you bleeding?"

"I've been knifed. And before you run out the door and

try to figure out who did it, it was completely my fault. I shouldn't have stepped in where I wasn't needed." He asked him what had happened as he retrieved his first aid kit. "Two women fighting. Like fists and hair pulling fighting. I thought I should help before someone got hurt. Well, it turned out they weren't fighting. I have no idea what they thought they were doing when one of them had a bloody nose and the other looked like a rat had taken up a home in their hair."

"That doesn't explain how you were knifed." Sawyer hissed when he saw the long cut in his back. "You're not stabbed, little brother, but you do have a nice slice across your back. You want me to stitch it, or do you want to shift to heal up?"

"Shift. By the way, congratulations on moving home. I wish you the best of luck." Sawyer asked him why he'd say that. "I don't know if I could stay caged up in one place. It sounds too boring to me."

When Gunner went into the bathroom to shift and shower, Sawyer thought about what he was saying. Caged up would be a complaint from Gunner. He'd been in the service since he'd been eighteen. Ten years. Rarely did he seem to be home anymore.

None of them knew what he did for a living in the service, but it must have been pretty dangerous. Every few months or so he'd be hurt somehow, and would be sent home to recuperate. Not that he needed it, being a tiger, but Gunner took it where he could, he'd told him once.

"What is that smell?" He told Gunner it was his dinner. "That smells worse than the shit they give us in the mess hall. Let's go get a steak. My treat. Oh, before I forget to tell you, I've got six more weeks and I'm finished."

"Seriously? What brought this on?" Gunner told him that he didn't want to talk about it. "Okay, but you do know that I'm here if you ever want to. I bet Mom will be thrilled."

"No doubt, but don't tell her I'm home. I have a mission that I have to get back to, and I don't have a great deal of time to see her this trip. You know how she is. She can be pretty persuasive when she needs to be." Sawyer asked him if she'd try to keep him home. "No, but she will try and give me lots of food to take back with me. I don't have anywhere to store it anymore. I'm on the ground more than I am anywhere else, and never in one place for all that long."

"I won't tell her. I'm going home this weekend to help out around the house. Dad is feeling a lot better, Mom told me this morning." Gunner told him that he'd forgotten to ask. "It's all right. I know you've been busy. You've bled all over my couch."

He hadn't, but it was funny to see his brother jump up and check the seat. He and Gunner hadn't ever been close as children, but now that they were both older, they had really started to have fun together. Sawyer and Dwayne had always been close.

Dinner was fun. True to his word, Gunner paid and Sawyer left the tip. Their service was really good — he supposed that had a lot to do with Gunner being in uniform. Also, he could flirt better than anyone he knew.

Gunner left him about midnight. They had talked about everything, but really nothing at all. He was glad that he was leaving the service. Sawyer was worried that he had something bad to tell, and hoped that he'd let it go soon enough that it didn't fester. Gunner wasn't one to be vengeful, but he was harsh when he had to be.

Going to bed that night, he marked off his calendar that counted down how many more days he had to work. This weekend with his parents was going to be hard, because he knew that he'd only have a week to go. Some things, he told himself, were worth waiting for. And this was something that he'd waited for for a very long time. Being home all the time.

~*~

Raven counted to ten before she spoke to the woman across from her. Then she counted again. Her mother was going to drive her to drink, she knew it. When she felt like she could answer her without cursing, something that Raven did well and her mother hated, she finally spoke.

"Look. We've been over this time and time again. I'm not going to marry anyone that you pick out for me. I'm not going to marry the first man that comes along, either. I'm happy with the way things are for me—single and a mom. If you don't care for that, then we can stop having these combative lunches where you talk at me and not to me." Her mom, Merriam, huffed and said she was getting too old not to have a husband. "I don't need one. Molly and I are doing just fine."

"I'll cut you off then. How well will you live when I do that?" Raven just laughed. "What is it you find so funny?"

"I find you funny if you think that your money, which I haven't gotten from you in ten years, will make squat of a difference to us." She picked at her salad, and wished now that she'd ordered the hamburger that she'd wanted. "I have money. A good deal of it. If you'll remember, Grandfather and Grandmother left me their estates and their holdings. Molly is in a good school that she loves. The house, Grandmother's, is perfect for us. We don't need you cutting off something that we've never had."

11

"Why are you so obstinate? You have been since before you were born." Here we go, Raven thought. The story of her birth. "I was in labor for two days with you. And you were six days late. Always stubborn. Then, if that wasn't enough, you had to be the biggest baby the doctor had ever seen."

"You know, I looked that up. An eight pound baby is not all that big, Mother. Your story gets larger than life every time you tell it. Molly weighed in at nine pounds ten ounces, and I don't ever plan to hold that over her head. Why don't you come up with something different?" Mother huffed again. "Look, I've told you this before. I'm happy. Why do you think that having a husband will make me any more so? Is it because I have Molly? You don't still think I should have married her father, do you? Christ Mother, he was married already. When I had the affair with him, I didn't know, besides, you know as well as I do that he died before he even knew I was pregnant. I got Molly out of it, so it wasn't all terrible."

"My friends at the club talk about you being an unwed mother. I just don't care for it." Raven ate two bites of her salad and shoved it away. She called for their waiter. "What are you doing? That is good for you. You need to eat better before you end up looking like the side of a cow."

"Thank you so much, Mother." When the waiter nearly smiled, she winked at him. "I'll have a cheeseburger with everything on it, well done. Fries, and please bring me a chocolate malt. Not shake, malt. If I'm going to be a cow or the side of one, I should have more dairy."

"You're embarrassing me, Raven Addington. I will not have it." Raven told her mother that she didn't care at the moment. "I'm going to tell your father what you did to me."

"I didn't do anything to you, and I'm twenty-nine years

old. The last time I looked, I was too old for my dad to care if I was eating a burger or not. In fact, I think he'd want to join me." Her mother's mouth looked pinched. Raven wanted to comment on it, but her grandma on her dad's side sat down in the empty chair next to her. "I didn't know you were coming, Grandma Holly. What brings you here?"

"I saw you two in the window and thought that you might need rescuing from your mother. But I can see by the look on her face that you're winning this round. Hello, Merriam. How's life treating you? Still on that blasted diet?" Raven's malt was set in front of her. "Oh my, I'd love one of those too. And if I know my granddaughter, she's having something wonderful to go with it. Whatever she's having, bring me one too."

"She's eating fatty foods, and it's going to make her fat again, Holly. You mustn't encourage her." Grandma Holly waved Mother off.

"Why do you equate me being pregnant with being fat? I bet you didn't gain an ounce when you were pregnant, did you?" Mother told her that was a vulgar conversation. "Vulgar? Mother, just what century were you born in?"

Mother got up and left her and Grandma Holly there. It was all right with Raven; she was tired of trying to appease her anyway. Grandma Holly asked about Molly.

"She's doing well. Today is her last day of school, so she's home tomorrow. Margo is going to drop her off here when they're finished up for the day. So if you stay with me, you'll get to see her yourself." She said that she was having lunch with her favorite people today. "Thank you. I haven't any idea why Mother insists that we have these luncheons weekly. She never is satisfied with my life. Mother said I should be married. That I was embarrassing her at the club. I also am going to be cut off from her money if I don't marry soon. I had to tell her once again that I don't want a husband."

"Of course you don't. I loved your grandda more than I did anyone. But after he died, I started having fun again. I didn't realize what a fuddy duddy he was." They both laughed. Grandma had grieved hard for Grandda when he passed away. It took Molly being born to bring her out of it. "I would like to ask you a favor. I'm going on a trip next month, and I'd like to take you and Molly with me."

"I can't, not next month. I have a lot of meetings about the merger that I'm doing. It'll make you and I a great deal of money once it goes through." Grandmother said that she had plenty. "Yes, I'm sure you do, but this will help a great many people. The company that I'm acquiring is coming apart at the seams. Last month they had to lay off about two hundred people. I'm hoping that we'll be able to hire those people back and hire more before I'm finished. With the building and the people, I'll have more people for sorting and sizing. It will make our clothing business larger than we had anticipated."

Molly joined them, hugging her like she'd not just seen her this morning. Grandmother got extra hugs because it had been three days since Molly had seen her. Grandmother asked if Molly could go with her.

"It's up to her. What do you say, Molly, my dear? Do you want to go with your old great grandmother on a trip? Where are you going anyway?" She told her. "Oh well, Paris and Scotland sounds very good. I can't think that you'd want to go on a trip like that."

"Yes, of course I would." Molly was the oldest eleven-year-old that Raven had ever seen. She worried like an old person, studied like she was never going to learn anything, and could speak four languages, thanks mostly to Raven having to travel all the time. "How long will we be gone? Misha is having a birthday party, and I'd very much like to miss it. Her mom is friends with Grandma Addington."

"Why do you want to miss that?" Molly just rolled her eyes at Raven. "I see. I should have known it merited eye rolling when you said that she was friends with Mother." Molly laughed. "You're going to still have to get her a gift. So don't forget to go shopping with me."

"I'll take her. She's going to need new things for our trip. We'll be gone for two weeks. I have some business deals that I have to take care of there, which won't take that long, then you and I can have a bit of fun." Molly, of course, was all for going with GGMa, she called her. "Also, don't worry about a thing, Raven. I don't get her all to myself often, and I want to have a lot of fun."

After they left the restaurant, she went back to work and Molly and her GGMa went shopping. Raven did wish that she could go with them, but things were getting too heated up around her buying out this company, and she wanted to make sure that it went through for a great many people.

Raven did miss male company. She'd not been on a date since before Molly had been born. And now that she could leave her daughter alone for a few hours, she didn't remember how to find a date to go out with. She wasn't into a long term or even a permanent relationship. In fact, she'd rather never have anything that was even semi long term.

When seven o'clock rolled around, she was still at her desk going over paperwork. She wanted to go home, put her feet up, and enjoy a free night. It had been so long since she'd had one of those, Raven wasn't sure that she remembered how it worked.

At nine, she called it a day and gathered up her purse and her briefcase to go home. Of course she was the only one in the parking lot at that hour, and the lights were on half-light by then. It was to save money, she knew, but it was creepy in the garage when all the corners were dark.

The flash of movement had her falling to the concrete flooring. Raven hit her head on the car door as she went down. Something hit her again, and Raven curled into a ball to try and keep from being hurt more. But whoever it was, they were determined to beat her to death, she thought.

After what seemed like hours of someone hurting her with something hard, they began kicking her in the ribs and in the head. Raven was sick with pain—her body had to be broken. When it stopped, Raven laid there waiting for it to start again. Hoping that it was finished, Raven pulled her cell phone.

She knew that she only had to press three buttons to get help, but for the life of her, she didn't remember which buttons it was. Her hand that was holding the cell phone was covered in blood. The use of her fingers was difficult too. Finally remembering what she needed to do, she got a dispatcher on the phone.

"My name is Raven Addington. I work at the Addington Building on Tenth. I've been attacked. I'm bleeding." The dispatcher asked her if the assailant was gone. "I think so. I can't see very well either. I'm by my car. My car is blue. I hurt so badly. Can you please send someone to help me?"

"Help is on the way, Miss Addington. Just stay on the line with me, all right?" Raven started crying. "We'll help you, honey. You just hang on for a little while. I have four cars in the area, and they'll be able to help you. An ambulance is on its way. Do you need me to call anyone?"

Did she? Raven couldn't think beyond how hard it was for her to breathe, how her head hurt so badly that even blinking hurt. She must have said this aloud, because the dispatcher told her she was sorry, and that she would be in a hospital soon.

"My grandmother. She has my daughter. I can't remember the number." She asked if it was in her phone. "Yes, but I can't see anything. I have been hurt in my head."

"Raven, you should be able to hear the ambulance and police now. Can you?" She said she thought that she did. "Good girl. When they get there, ask one of the officers to call your grandma for you, all right? I'll tell him as well, but you remind him when he gets there. His name is Sawyer. He's one of the good guys."

"I hurt." She said that she knew she did.

Raven must have passed out for a bit, because when she woke up this time, she could hear the voices of three men talking over her. She could hear their different voices. Screaming and knocking out at them, she heard a calming voice from behind her saying they were there to help her. "I need someone to call my grandma. Please, will someone do — The dispatcher said that someone named Sawyer would do it."

"I've called her for you. She is going to meet you at the hospital. Mrs. Addington said to make sure that I told you that she's not calling your mother until you're there." Thanking him, she heard someone ask her if she was allergic to anything. Almost the second that she said no, she felt the

17

pinch of a needle, then nothing more.

Chapter 2

Sawyer had been called in to do another shift tonight, his last night on the job, and he was nearly to the end of it when the call had come in about Ms. Addington. As soon as he got out of the cruiser he knew that she was in bad shape. There was so much blood around her that he didn't think she'd make it long enough to have the medics help her. But she not only surprised him with that, but also that she was clear enough to ask about her grandmother.

"You wait here for the grandmother and mother, and I'll do the paperwork for this. You really saved my ass tonight, Bishop. Thanks for coming in." Sawyer said that he could use the overtime. "You bet. I guess you'll be leaving soon too."

"Yeah, I'm driving home tonight. Which reminds me, I left my clothes in the car. Can you bring them back in to me? After tonight I'm going to go home and live with my parents for a little while until I can get something closer to home." He asked how far home was now. "Only about forty minutes, but it's a bitch with highway traffic. I'm not getting any younger, you know." Paul was still laughing when he left him there.

Raven had arrived about twenty minutes ago, and Sawyer was still waiting for the grandmother. Sawyer knew who she was the moment that she walked in the door. The little girl surprised him, but he made his way to her when he heard the older woman ask about Raven.

"I'm the responding officer. I was told to give you whatever information you needed." She asked where Raven was. "She's in surgery, and will be for a bit longer. They have two surgeons working on her. She was beaten up badly."

Sawyer glanced at the little girl, and knew that she was stressed out with worry. Looking at Deb, who ran the emergency room desk, he asked if she could take the child—Molly, he found out—to the nurses' station to let her rest up.

"Only for you, Sawyer, you know that." He smiled at her and looked at the older woman again. "She's gonna be awhile, Mrs. Addington, so I'll just keep an eye on little Molly here for you."

"Thank you." Mrs. Addington looked at him. "I'm not a spring chicken, young man, so you tell me what happened to Raven and don't be going around the bushes about it. I'm sick with worry, and I have to call her momma yet. A woman that will make it sound as if all this is Raven's fault, and that she should have been more careful or some shit. It's always about Merriam."

"I was told that you'd want it straight. The best we can tell is that Raven was hit multiple times with a ball bat first, then kicked repeatedly afterwards. The reason that I could tell that is because the footprints spread out the blood when she was kicked. Robbery wasn't the motive, as her car wasn't taken even though the keys were right there. Her purse and her briefcase were lying next to her as well." She—Holly, he was told to call her—asked what it could have been. "I don't know as yet. The police are working on the details now. The ball bat was left behind, so hopefully they can get some prints off it. And there were security cameras around the place as well."

"She's had some trouble with a couple of employees of late. I don't have their names on me now, but I'll call our attorney to have him get them. Raven keeps very detailed notes on such things." He said that would help. "What are you not telling me, Sawyer? I can take it."

"She coded twice when she was being brought in. The first time, I was told they didn't think she was going to come out of it. The second was minor, but no less important to note. May I ask you a question? You don't have to answer it, but I was just curious." She said that he shouldn't be surprised by the answer. "I'm assuming that Raven is a great deal like you—strong and stubborn, outspoken, and a little on the tense side. Is she married?"

"No. She's never been married. Molly is her daughter, eleven years old, but the man she was having a fling with had traded out her birth control pills for fake ones so that she'd carry his child. The moron. He thought that if Raven would have his child then he could get a nice big divorce from his current wife, marry Raven, then get all her money. My granddaughter is very rich. Then about a week after she found out she was going to have a baby, sperm donor was killed in a bank robbery. Not him doing the robbery, but he was killed all the same. He never knew about Molly." She looked at him with a squint in her eyes. "Why do you ask?"

"I'm a shifter. A white Bengal tiger. You know of shifters."

Holly said that she had several working for her. "I'm her mate. Raven, she's my mate. To be honest, Holly, I haven't the slightest clue what I'm to do now. I am not even on the same class level as she is."

"I don't understand that, but please don't tell her mother." He said that he wasn't going to tell anyone else, but that he had needed to tell someone. "You picked the right person, young man. I have to call her mother about Raven being hurt. I'd very much like it if you hung around here for a while. I don't know who it is that hurt Raven, but they might be back to finish the job. Can you do that?"

"As of midnight, I'm finished being a cop. I gave my notice two weeks ago. So you know, I cannot help you in a police situation. All right?" Holly said she was all right with that, so long as he could use a gun if it came to that. "Yes, ma'am, I can do that part. My buddy, he left me my clothing. I was driving home tonight instead of tomorrow. But I'll stay here with you. Just give me a few minutes to change out of these and into my civilian clothing."

While Sawyer was in the bathroom, he reached out to his mom. She was disappointed that he might be a couple of more days, but he told her that he'd be home forever after that. He didn't mention that he'd found his mate. Honestly, he wasn't sure what to say to anyone about having her. Instead, he told his mom how much he loved her.

I love you too, Sawyer. Your brothers arrived about an hour ago. It's so nice that I'll be having all of you so close again. You just do what you have to do, and drive carefully on your way home. She laughed a little. *You are going to be surprised by how much better your dad looks even since last weekend. I'm so glad that he can get out into the sun. It makes him feel less confined, too.*

I'll let you know what I'm doing here. As I said, there has been a beating, and the grandmother to the girl asked me to hang around for a couple of days until the police make some progress on her being hurt. Mom wished them luck, and said to hurry the police along. *Yes, I want them to as well.*

When he found Holly, she was up on the second floor where the operating rooms were. It would take a while, he'd been told, so he asked if either of them wanted anything to eat or drink. Molly said she'd like a drink, and Holly declined.

"Sawyer, Merriam is on her way in. Why don't you take Molly down to the cafeteria with you so that she doesn't have to witness her?" He asked if she trusted him. "If I didn't, you'd not be here at all. She'll be just fine with you. You can get to know her a little too."

He wasn't so sure about that, but Molly followed him to the elevator. When they stepped on, there were other people on the lift, so Molly put her hand into his bigger one and leaned closer to him. Sawyer didn't know what to do—he'd never held a little kid's hand before—but she seemed okay so he didn't say anything.

The kitchen was open now, so he asked her if she wanted something to eat. Sawyer told her that he'd not eaten in a while, and was going to have something. Molly ordered a kids' meal and a chocolate milk. He, however, ordered a large breakfast with white milk.

"You don't have to impress me. I don't care." Sawyer asked her why she thought he was trying to impress her. "My mom is rich, and people are always being nice to me because they think I can get them to date her. I don't do that. Mom says that she has her own mind, and that I should too. So you don't have to impress me."

23

"Believe it or not, I don't care how much money your mom has. I was there after she was hurt, and your grandma asked me to stick around in case the people who did this to her return." He drank down his milk and got up to get him another one. When he returned, she was still sitting there doing nothing. "Aren't you hungry anymore? Does being nasty make you ill?"

"I wasn't nasty to you." He just stared at her. "I wasn't. You're rude, and I don't like you one bit. And when you ask my mom out, I'm going to tell her not to do it. She'll listen to me. We're very close."

"Again, I don't care. I'm here for your grandma. If you'll remember, I didn't make the plans for us to have breakfast together. I'm a former cop, and she thought that you all would be safer with me around. However, I've just come to realize that if anyone came around, you could just be rude and nasty to them and they'd just leave you alone." He ate two bites of his eggs before he continued. "You must be a great deal like your grandma Merriam. Holly said that she was a rude person who thought that everything was all about her."

Molly didn't say anything while he finished his breakfast. When he got up to take his tray back, he asked her if she was finished. When she shook her head no, that she wasn't, he got himself a bagel and cream cheese to eat while she decided what she was going to do with her breakfast. She was eating when he returned.

"My mom is all I have besides my grandmas. I don't like spending time with Grandma Merriam. She fusses at me a lot, like about my hair and my clothing. Mom said that I have my own style, and she didn't care if I wore what I wanted at home, but when we go out, I have to dress nicely." He said that his mom said that too. "Why are you a former policeman?"

"I got tired of arresting the same people over and over. Not always the same people, really, but the same type of people. My partner was shot a couple of weeks ago, and I had enough." He pulled out his phone and showed her the picture of his family. "I have five brothers and my parents. My dad has been ill, but he's getting better now. I miss them."

"I don't have any brothers or sisters. I think I like that. I get Mom all to myself when she's not working too much." He said that he was working too much as well. "You and my mom—you can date her if you want."

"I don't want to. I'm just a poor cop that has no money at all. I'd not even know of a place to take her even if I did ask her out." Molly told him that her mom loved the zoo. "That's not really a date, is it? I mean, I don't know. It's been a long time since I've been on a date anyway. Are you finished? If so, what do you think I can take back for your grandmas? I don't want them to be hungry when there is no reason for it."

"GGMa would love a Danish. Grandma Merriam won't eat anything here, because she'll say that it has too many germs for her to ingest. She's very picky too. Even pizza isn't something that she'll eat unless the cook makes it for us." Molly just rolled her eyes, and Sawyer laughed. "It's not the same thing. Having a hot pizza brought to you is so cool. Mom said it's the thrill of waiting for it."

"I agree on that one. I love a meat pizza when I can afford it. Or maybe a big meatball sub. My mom, she can make the best meatballs. She always makes a lot of them so we can have subs the next time we get together." Molly said that was nice. Grandma Merriam didn't eat red meat. "Really? Red meat is the best for people like me."

"You're not human, are you?" He said that he was a tiger, a white one. "I've never seen a white tiger except at the zoo. They look so sad there."

"They more than likely are. I knew a shifter once who was in one of those traveling zoos that has tricks and rides. He said that he loved being there. He could rest when he wanted, and so long as he didn't hurt anyone, they kept him fed and well cared for. That was all he wanted after his mate passed away." She asked if mates were like boyfriends. "More like a husband and wife. Our kind, we only have one chance at happiness, and we love hard and fast. I think because we're cats. I don't know."

"Slippery, our cat, was always having kittens. They must not mate for life, I don't think." Sawyer laughed, and said that was a different kind of cat. "I guess you're much bigger. Than a cat."

"By a great deal. Are you ready to get GGMa some food and take it back to her?" Molly asked if she could have a Danish too, for later. "Sure. Want some milk to go with it?"

He had to count out his change to finish paying for the meals. Sawyer had a few bucks in the bank. He was going home soon, and would need to find himself a job.

Getting off the elevator, he heard the women. They were not having a good conversation.

"Molly, honey, I want you to stay behind me, all right? I don't want you hurt in case GGMa throws something."

Molly laughed and said that she'd go to the nurses' station. As soon as she was safe, he walked to the two women and whistled as loudly as he could. That got their attention. The younger woman, he knew by her looks, was Merriam. Holly turned and smiled at him, but it was tight, like she was very pissed off.

"Did you have a nice meal, Sawyer?" He told Holly yes, and that the company wasn't too bad either. "Good. Oh, is that for me? I love Danish. I know that it's not the best for—"

"It's not the best for anyone. Why do you continue to eat that sort of thing when you know that it's fattening?" Holly didn't answer her, but sat down. Molly came to sit with her GGMa and ate her Danish as well. "What do you think you're doing? You will not eat that in front of me. Give it to me right now."

"No." He didn't know why he was intruding, but when Holly and Molly both looked at him with their mouths open, he did the only thing he could think of—try and make the woman see reason. "Her mom is hurt, and her grandmother has been taking care of her since they arrived. She deserves a treat. I think you should just sit down and not worry about a few calories at the moment. Everyone is stressed out."

He saw the moment that she was going to strike him. Instead of letting her, like he should have, he grabbed her hand and held it in his own. Sawyer had never seen boiling over anger before today, and this woman, Merriam, was just seething with it.

"I'm a cop, and if you hit me, I'm going to have to arrest you for hitting an officer." He didn't think that this one little lie would be too bad. It might even calm her down some. "Now, as I suggested before, go over there and sit your skinny ass down."

~*~

Holly loved the young man. Sawyer had given up going home to stay with them, as she had asked him to. Molly was better around him too. At first she'd told her that she didn't

27

like him, that he was a slob. Holly had scolded her for saying such a thing when he'd been covered in blood and dirty. She told her that some people had to get dirty in order to make a living. That she was ashamed of her for making such a statement.

After they'd come back from eating, Molly seemed a great deal more relaxed around Sawyer, and she would ask him questions. That had been four days ago. They both were avoiding Merriam like she had some awful disease that they were afraid of contracting.

Holly found herself an empty patient's room to make a call. She wanted some answers that she knew only one person could get for her. Pulling out her cell, she called her attorney, Brooks Hall.

"Hello, Brooks. I need a couple of things from you. If you're not too busy." He said that he was never too busy for her. "Thank you. I should have done this days ago but I was just so worried about Raven and Molly. If you could, I need the names of the people that Raven had to fire recently—say within the last six months or so. Also, I have a young man here that was with Raven after she was injured. I want you to do a complete background check on him and his family. His name is Sawyer Bishop. I don't know anything else about him other than he's recently quit his job as a police officer close to the hospital."

"I've heard of him. I don't remember where just now, but I'll have something for you in about a half hour—sooner if I can manage it. How is our little girl doing?" She told him what she knew. "That poor thing. Have the police found out anything? I know the paper said very little about her, but you said it wasn't robbery."

"Sawyer is keeping tabs on it for me. I like this young man, Brooks. And he's mate to Raven." She heard him laugh, a short bark of it. "Yes, sometimes I think we have the same mind. She's not going to be happy if he decides to do anything about it. He's saying that he's not good enough for her. Damned boy. You should have seen him take on Merriam. And Molly is very attached to him."

"I don't think that it works that way, Holly. Let me get back to you on that as well, all right?" She said that would be fine. "Do you ladies need anything? Something to do for Molly? I just had a thought. You know what you should do? Have him take Molly home with him. You told me the other day that he was missing his family get together. Do that for them both. I don't know how you'll do it, but I have faith in you."

"I love that idea, Brooks. My goodness, this might work out better than I thought. I really like him, so I hope you don't find anything bad in his background. I might just have to hire someone to take him out of his life." Brooks told her not to say such things. "Why not? I'm an old woman. I'd no more kill anyone than I would kiss a horse. Oh, I just remembered something. He told me that he's a white Bengal tiger. That should help some."

"I've written down everything. And I'll get back to you. If you need anything, you just let me know. I'll be there in no time."

After thanking him, she joined her son, Roger, and daughter-in-law Merriam, along with Sawyer and Molly. Sitting down, she wondered what she'd do if Raven left her too.

She'd lost her husband about the time that Raven had

found out that she was carrying a dead man's child. Raven hadn't been sure that she wanted the baby—giving it up for adoption seemed the best for her. But Holly had begged her to keep it, that she'd help her with the little girl. Then after Molly was born, it was as if every second Holly had been contemplating death and joining her husband was all washed away. All it had taken was the baby to grab her finger and Holly was in love.

Merriam, of course, was a different story all together. She had told Raven that keeping the child would guarantee her never getting a decent man to marry her. Whatever that meant. Merriam had liked Scott, Molly's biological father. And then she'd ranted about Raven being fat, then too fat as the months went on. Finally, Raven had moved out, and had settled that quickly.

There hadn't been any offer of babysitting from her mother. Merriam told Raven that she'd gotten herself into the mess she was in, and that she'd just have to deal with it. Holly would watch Molly everyday if she was allowed. Now that the child was older, it was absolutely wonderful to take her places, have conversations with her. Molly was a smart child. It was too bad that Merriam had pushed the child away from the very start.

Roger, her son, wasn't like that, but he didn't do anything to bring Molly into his life and home. He would give into his wife whenever she put her foot down about anything. The trials with Molly were no different. If he wanted to spend time with his granddaughter, he would come to her house and do that. But he would leave much too soon for her tastes, and leave behind a child that thought for sure that her other grandparents didn't love her.

The more she thought about Molly and Sawyer together, Holly knew that Merriam would crumble if she saw them together. At least she hoped so. Raven needed a good strong man in her corner in dealing with life. Or just having a life would be good for her too.

Her cell was ringing just as she was about to ask Sawyer to do her a favor. When she saw Brooks's face there, she went back to the empty room and closed the door this time. If she had to curse, she didn't want everyone to hear it.

"I knew that I knew his name. He's not only a retired cop, Holly, but a decorated one. Several times since becoming a police officer, he's saved lives in a burning home. Twice he put a victim in his cruiser and rushed him to the hospital when an ambulance wouldn't have made it there in time. He was also decorated with the highest honor that an officer can get. He's gotten the Public Safety Officer Medal of Valor twice in his career, Holly. Quite an honor for someone as young as him." She was happy to hear that. Holly asked about his family. "He comes from a good home. Mother and father are still married and have six sons. They are barely making it on what the boys send them monthly, but each of them do it religiously every time they get paid. The father was sick recently, and each of them rushed home to see to him, then have been there whenever they can to help out around the house. The middle son—fourth, I believe—is just as highly decorated in the service. Whatever he does, it's very hush hush. They're all very good men, and they love their parents a great deal."

"That's wonderful news. Thank you so much." He interrupted her good news for something different. "You said that you knew something about mates. What is it?"

"Once they find their mates, especially tigers — any cats, really — they are mated for life. Which is good. But if they find their mates and don't do anything about it, like ignore them for some reason — in Sawyers case, Raven's money — then they go mad with the need to be around them. In the background, so to speak. But they have to be put down like a mad dog would be. It's not pretty." She told him she didn't want that to happen. "Neither do I. This is the best man for her. While he's very quiet, I was told, he does have the ability to make people shut up when he needs it."

Holly told him about Sawyer putting Merriam in her place. "I wish I would have thought to have my camera out. But I was too busy defending Raven. I don't know what she has against that girl, but I have to tell you, Brooks, I wanted to hit her badly." He begged her not to do that. "I won't. At least where anyone could see me."

He laughed, and she thought he thought she was kidding. But of late, Holly was tempted to hurt Merriam any way that she could. The damned woman was pushing away the two most precious things in her life — a child and a grandchild. Perhaps Sawyer could bring them all together. And if he couldn't, then he'd be there to stand up for them both. Holly thought that they needed that more than anything.

Chapter 3

Sawyer didn't think this was such a good idea. Molly was a good kid and he loved spending time with her, but taking her to his house made him think that his parents and brothers were going to jump to the wrong conclusion. The right one, really, but wrong if they thought that he was going to have anything to do with Raven.

"My brothers are all big men. My dad too, but he's been sick. You'll like my mom. She's the best cookie and pie baker in the world as far as I'm concerned." She told him she was excited to see the tractors. "They're being used a great deal this time of year, so if my mom thinks you'll be okay on the big things, you can have a ride on one of them."

"Really? Can you take my picture? My mom will want to see it when she wakes up." Molly had gotten to see her mom before they left. He'd not been so sure about that either, but Molly wanted to tell her mom goodbye and to tell her that she'd be back. "You don't want me to meet your parents, do you, Sawyer?"

"I do. I think that they'll fall head over heels in love with you. My dad, he loves little girls." That didn't come out right, but he thought that trying to fix it would only make it worse. Sawyer was making big mistakes here, and had not a clue how to fix them. "I didn't tell them that you were coming, just in case you changed your mind. Mom is making a big meal for all of us because she's wanted us all to come—"

"Sawyer, are you nervous?" He nodded. "I'll be on my best behavior. I promise you. GGMa packed me some clothing to wear outside. She said that I should have play clothes if I was going to a farm." That was another thing. Holly seemed to know a great deal about the farm that his parents ran. But he didn't say anything to Molly.

"I'm not worried about you not being a good girl, Molly. I'm really not. But we're a big loud family that talks over each other, and we only use one fork and one spoon when we eat." She giggled. "Yeah, I'm not making any sense, am I? I'm sorry. I'm very nervous, as you've pointed out. I don't want to make any of your family upset with me if you scrape your knee or something like that."

"I've cut my knees before. They always mend. You have to chill out or you're going to have a heart attack. That's what happened to my GGPa. He was so stressed out all the time that he didn't relax. You might...Mom called it blow a gasket. I don't know what that means, but I don't want you to do that." He said that he didn't either. "Okay then. If I break an arm or something, you can freak out. But don't sweat the little stuff. My GGMa tells me that all the time. I do know what that means."

"Good. If I can, I'll show you what a gasket is on the tractor. One of my brothers was on it when that happened once. They would have a better story to tell you about it. They curse. I do too, but I've been trying to curb it while around you." She giggled again. "Molly, my dear, I think that I could love you forever. All right. Here's the driveway. Last chance to have me take you back."

"Nope, I'm ready to eat some down home cooking. Some pie and cookies. And to ride on a tractor. You are going to be all right, Sawyer." She patted him on the arm as they pulled up in front of the house. "You still have my GGMa's credit card, right? So that if I need clothing for something, you can get it?"

"I do. I don't think you'll need it, but I have it." Mom came out on the porch, followed by Gunner. "That's Gunner and my mom. Gunner will be carrying a gun and a knife. I think he wears it to bed. So don't be afraid of him, all right?"

"I'm not. So long as you're with me."

She got out of the car before he could. Running up on the porch, she stood there in front of Gunner. Neither of them said anything as Sawyer got out of the car, so he went to the trunk and got their bags. He watched the three of them.

"My name is Molly Addington. You're Gunner." Gunner went down to her level and said that she was right. "You're very tall to me, but I guess that's all right. Do you work for the government?"

"Yes. Why are you here?" She told him. "I see. So your mom is the lady that was hurt, and Sawyer thought that bringing you here would be a good thing? Why? Are we supposed to have you for dinner"

"Gunner, don't scare her. My name is Sippy. Well, it's Serendipity, but everyone calls me Sippy. Is your momma doing better?" Molly told his mom that she was still resting.

35

"Poor lamb. I do hope that you're hungry. I've made a lot of food. Not that it won't be eaten, but I want to make sure you get something." The two of them went into the house holding hands.

"You brought a little girl here. Are you insane? She'll be scarred for life after this." Sawyer told him what was going on. "I can see that, Sawyer, but I'm not the kind of person that hangs out with kids. I don't think any of us are."

"She'll be fine. She's a great deal stronger than she looks. And has a bit of a temper too, so don't fuck with her." He said that Mom seemed to like her. "She's not a hulking man with more testosterone then any ten men that we know. Of course she likes her."

"I'm glad that you're home. Anything you want to tell me about this kid? Or her mother?" Sawyer said nothing. "I see. Well that does make things a little different, doesn't it? Will the mom live?"

"Yes, I believe so. She's getting stronger daily, and the doctor said that was a good sign. They're keeping her in a medically induced coma so that she won't be in so much pain." Gunner nodded. "Am I going to get a hug or what? I mean, I am bringing home a little girl for you to scare to death."

Gunner hugged him and they entered the big house. The rest of them were there, sitting in the living room watching television, some black and white movie about cowboys. He said hi as he walked by the room and got several grunts. Going to the kitchen, where he knew Mom would have headed, he found Molly and his mom cutting into a pie. Apple, if he didn't miss his bet.

"Oh my goodness, Sawyer, you were right. This is the best

pie I've ever eaten. And your mom said that I could call her Sippy. Isn't that a cool name?" Molly ate another bite before drinking some of her milk. "I'm to sleep in your room, and you have to bunk on the couch since you didn't tell anyone that I was coming. I love your mom, Sawyer."

"So do I." He hugged and kissed his mom before asking where Dad was. "I'll take Molly to go and see him. If that's all right."

"It is." He took Molly off the stool she'd been on, and Mom stopped him by saying his name. "I'm not as dense as you might think I am. You've found her, haven't you? And this little girl is...well, you know what she is to me."

"Yes, but don't get too attached, Mom. I'm sorry, but it'll never work out between us. They're about as far in the direction of being rich as we are being poor." She said his name again. "I'll talk to you later, Mom. I want to see Dad. Okay?"

"Yes, but you're wrong if you think this will end it. You know what I mean."

He nodded and left the kitchen. He didn't want to think a thing about what ignoring Raven would mean for him. Instead, he was going to introduce Molly to his dad. But again, Molly beat him to it.

"How are you feeling, Mr. Saul? I'm Molly Addington. My mom is in the hospital, and I've come for a visit to keep my mind off of it. Do adults really think that works?" Dad looked up at him and smiled at Molly. "You smile just like Sawyer. With your whole face. It's very nice."

"Thank you, young lady. That's the best news that you could give an old man." She told him that he wasn't old. He looked way younger than her Grandma Merriam. "Well, I

37

don't think that I'd say that to her if I were you. It might make her upset."

"She doesn't like me." Again Dad looked at Sawyer before Molly spoke again. "She didn't want Mom to keep me so that she could marry a nice man. I guess nice men don't want kids that they didn't make."

"You're very outspoken, aren't you?" Molly smiled at him. "Yes, that's the best way to get out of an argument or anything with me. Just that pretty smile. Why don't you and I have a walk around the barn? There are some new kittens out there. They're too young to take from their momma, but you can pet them."

"I'd like that, Mr. Saul." They were out the door before Sawyer could get a hug from his dad, or even a "Good to see you, son." Women. They would come between the best of men.

"Sawyer, you have a phone call." He moved out of the library that his dad had claimed as his own long ago. Going to the kitchen where there was a house phone, he picked up the phone and said hello. If he'd been at work he would have just said his last name, but his mom hated that.

"Sawyer, this is Rose Marie Conley. Do you remember me?' He said that he did not. "You and I went to high school together."

"No, I'm sorry. I don't remember you." His mother smacked him with her towel. "Perhaps if you can describe yourself, that might help me."

"I have blue eyes, brown hair." Just like every other person that he knew. "We went to prom our senior year. You drove my dad's car."

"I'm sorry, Ms. Conley, but that's not possible." She got

nasty with him then, and told him that she had pictures of them together. "Perhaps you might be thinking of someone else. I graduated from high school when I was thirteen, and I wasn't able to drive anything. I'm very sorry." The line went dead.

"I've had two of those calls this week. I wonder what's going on. Did you win some money and not tell me about it?" Sawyer kissed his mom on the cheek and told her that she'd be the first person that he told. "Tell me about this girl. Molly's mother. Do you know her?"

"No, not at all. I was the first on scene when she was hurt. I guess she's very wealthy, and very smart. I've not spoken to her other than to explain to her that she was going to be all right and that I called her grandmother." She asked about Molly. "Now there is someone that I could easily love. She's smart and friendly. That is, so long as you're not trying to date her mom. She doesn't have a very high opinion of men, I don't think. Molly's mom has been burnt before."

"I'm assuming that you brought Molly here so that we could meet her."

Sawyer told her that her grandmother wanted her to get out of the hospital for a while. To go someplace where she'd have some fun. "I have no idea why she thought bringing her here would accomplish that."

Mom smacked him again with her dishtowel. He looked out in the barn and saw Molly sitting on Dad's lap atop the tractor. When he pointed it out to his mom, she went out with her camera. She didn't say a word about him overextending himself, but told them both to pose so she could take a picture. The rest of his family came out too.

His brothers were falling all over themselves showing

Molly things. Mom had probably told them what she was to him. Nothing as far as he was concerned, but Molly was having such a good time that he didn't tell them that it wasn't going to work out.

When Mom called them all in to eat, Molly was as dirty as the rest of them were. Her face was smudged with something. Her hair was no longer in a neat plait, and she was grinning from ear to ear. It was her pretty dress that he was the most concerned with.

"It's all right, Sawyer, it's just a little dirt. I can get that out." He nodded at his mom. "She's going to need something besides little dresses if she's going to be hanging around here much. Do you have any shorts or tennis shoes, Molly?"

"No. I have some nice jeans, but they're not going to work either. They're all spangled up like I like them. I haven't any tennis shoes either. Just these. I think GGMa forgot to think about those." Mom told her that she'd take care of her tomorrow. "I have her credit card—Sawyer does. She told him to use it to get me stuff if I needed it."

"I think we can make do with what we have here. I have a sewing bag of the boys old clothing. No tennis shoes, but I think I might have kept Sawyer's old cowboy boots. Couldn't get them off him at bath time, either." Molly laughed when he turned red. "Let's get this supper on the table and eat. You and I will figure out something here in a bit. All right?"

"Yes, ma'am." The table was groaning as all the foot was put on it. Everyone had to wash up, and Molly joined him at the outdoor sink to do that with the rest of them. "I'm already having so much fun here. What do you have to do tomorrow?"

"Mom wants us to pick the fruit from the trees so she can make some jam." She asked if she really made her own jam. "She does. Mom also makes all her own juices, as well as putting up green beans and everything that we can plant in the garden. In a couple of months, we'll have pumpkins to give away to the townspeople. It's a big deal around here. Everyone comes out and picks out their pumpkins and brings their kids. Mom makes batches of cookies, and Dad makes the best cider in the county. I wish you could be here."

"Maybe Mom will be feeling better by then." He didn't say anything, knowing that her mom would want to be as far from him as she could be. "Am I cleaned up enough, Sawyer?"

"Yes, ma'am, you are. Let's get to eating." Mom had added an extra chair to the table and another plate by his. Molly was so excited, he thought she might make herself too sick to eat. But as things were passed by him, he asked her if she wanted any of whatever was on a platter or in a bowl. "You don't have to eat it all, honey. Just take what you want."

"I want to try everything. I bet it'll be the best food I've ever eaten."

Everyone laughed, and she did just what she'd said. Molly tried everything, even the hot pickles that Gunner loved. And surprisingly, she loved them as much as he did.

~*~

Molly felt like a different person as she walked around the farm with the rest of them. They were so nice to her that she wanted to hug them all the time. The boots that she'd put on this morning were a little hot, but she was told that this was hot work. Picking the apples off the tree was a lot harder than it looked.

Saul, as he asked her to call him, was sitting on the chair that one of them had brought out for him. Molly would take him an apple when he wanted one, and he'd cut it up and share it with her. The apples here tasted nothing like the ones from the store. They were so juicy that it ran down her arm when she ate it.

A man in an old van pulled up in front of where they were working. They all waved at him, asking about his family. When he sat down next to Saul on the ground, the two of them talked very seriously for some time. Then Wesley was told to put five bushels of apples in the back of his van. The man, Mr. Little, protested a little, but Molly could tell that he really wanted them. She listened as he stood there crying to Saul.

"You take them on home to your family, Mathew. Those kids of yours will have themselves a nice treat, and that wife of yours, she might bake you a pie or two from them." He asked him how much he wanted. "You know better than to ask me that. When a man gives you a gift you take it. And like I told you, you want to come over and help out tomorrow, you bring them kids of yours. Molly there, she'll enjoy getting dirty with them."

She knew that the Bishops didn't have much money. They didn't act like it, but she'd seen the bills that were past due when Sippy brought them in from the mailbox. Molly hadn't been snooping, but she just happened to see them. There were four of them this morning. Molly had a feeling that there would be more later. Yet Saul was giving away apples.

"Mr. Little doesn't have anything. His wife has been very ill for a long time, and sometimes he can't work like he should. So he lost his job." She nodded at Dwayne, another son of Saul's, when he told her that. She asked him about money. "Sometimes when you have a lot, like we do when it comes to food, you share it with someone else who might not have anything to feed their family. You should remember, Molly, that you never know what sort of situation that another person is in, so being nice and sharing is a good thing. Also, it makes Mr. Little feel better that my dad is allowing him to come here and work them off. But even if he doesn't work, Dad won't care a bit that he took the apples. Like he said, the kids will get a treat."

"You guys, you don't care that he gave away the apples that you picked either, do you?" Dwayne told her no, it made them feel good that their family could help someone in need. "You're all very nice, did you know that? I know some kids' parents from school that would never do that. Not even if they were dying from not having any food."

The van came back an hour later and a lady got out with Mr. Little. She was sickly and weak; Mrs. Little could barely walk to where Saul was. Mr. Little went back to his van and brought a big bag and handed to Saul. Then after they hugged again, Sippy came out with a bag and handed it to them. It looked like more food.

After they left a second time, lunch was called for them to come in and eat. Molly didn't know if she could do much more picking. She was about to bake in the clothing that she had on. But she didn't say a word. Molly was going to be as tough as the guys and pick until she dropped.

"Molly, Ms. Little sent you over some clothes that her kids have outgrown. After you eat, you try them on, and if they need taken in a little or something, I'll do that for you. No sense in burning up when you don't have to."

Lunch was as big as dinner had been the night before. Molly had it in her head to help clean up, but she was nearly falling asleep in her chair when pie was served. She didn't remember being carried up to Sawyer's bed, but she woke up feeling like she'd been sleeping on a cloud. His bed was much nicer than hers was.

There were not only shirts with short sleeves in the bag, but shorts too. They all fit her. And the tennis shoes were the most wonderful things she'd ever put on her feet, she thought after wearing those boots all morning. Molly danced around the kitchen when she had everything on to go back outside, and she was as excited about picking again as she'd been about coming here.

Two children on bikes came over about the time they were going to pick the grapes. She'd never had a bike, didn't even know how to ride one, so she was envious of the boy and the girl that were on them. Saul called her over and introduced her to the kids.

"This here is Todd Little, and that's his sister Jane. They came over to hang out with you for a little while." She asked about the grapes. "Ah, you go on now. And tomorrow I'll have Sawyer dig out one of those bikes that they had when they were kids. Do you know how to ride one?" Molly said no. "Then we'll work on that too. All right then."

Molly wasn't really shy, but she didn't know these kids, and her heart hurt for them. She knew that their momma was dying. Molly didn't know what she'd do if her mom were to die. When Jane took her hand into hers, Molly felt like she could like these children. They were nothing more than a girl and a boy that had come to play with her.

Jane wanted to see the kittens, and Molly felt great that she was able to show the little furballs to them. They were so adorable, and they'd only just gotten their eyes open. It occurred to her to ask about human eyes, and if hers had been open when she was born, but left that question to ask Sawyer. He seemed to know a lot about everything.

"You want me to teach you how to ride a bike? I can. It might get your knees a little banged up until you get used to it, but I sure can teach you." She asked Todd if it was hard. "Nah, not too hard. Like I said, you might get yourself banged up a bit, but it'll heal soon enough."

They spent the rest of the afternoon playing and teaching her how to ride a bike. Molly had to use Jane's bike, as it was smaller than Todd's, but after what seemed forever, she could pedal it round the driveway without falling over.

"You sure did take a long time. But after you got it going, you did all right." Molly thanked Jane and Todd for all their help. "Will Mrs. Bishop be upset with you about being all banged up like you are?"

"I don't think so. I have to go home tomorrow. My GGMa, she'll call them badges of honor because I learned something by getting them." He asked what GGMa was. "She's my great grandma. I have a regular grandma, but she wants me to call her Ms. Addington. I sometimes forget, but that's what she says."

"Is your momma getting better? Mine isn't. The doc told us that she was only going to be around for a few more weeks." Molly told Todd that she was sorry. "Me too. She's a good person, but we didn't have any money for insurance, so she didn't get to go to the doctor when she should have."

"I'm very sorry. If I could help you, I would." Jane said that she had helped them today by playing with them. "I'm glad that you came over. I don't get to play all that much with kids my own age. They're all snobby."

"All kids are snobby to us when they find out that we're

the Littles. But you have them pull out that bike for you this week, and I'll see to it for you if they don't have time." She thanked them both. "You're a good person, Molly. I'm so glad that we got to hang out with you today."

As they rode off, she thought that she'd made herself some very good friends. They were in need, and when her mom woke up, she was going to ask her if she could help them out with something. She didn't have any idea what that might be, but she'd ask.

Walking back to the house, now that she wasn't hanging out with her friends anymore, she felt every bump and cut on her body. She was trying really hard to be brave about it, but Molly thought that learning to ride a bike was much harder than picking apples. But it sure had been fun.

Sippy met her at the door and asked her if she was feeling all right. Nodding, she told her that she was only a little banged up. But she could ride a bike now.

"Well, if you ask me, I think it was well worth all those cuts, don't you?" She nodded, but could feel the pain coming on quicker now. "How about I run you a bath and you soak some of that soreness away? That way, when you get up tomorrow, you won't be nearly as sore. All right?"

Molly wrapped her arms around Sippy. Other than her GGMa and mom, she was the nicest person to her. When the tears started to fall, Sippy picked her up and held Molly tightly in her arms. It was one of the best hugs that she'd gotten in a very long time.

Chapter 4

Holly had to hide a smile every time she looked at little Molly. She knew that she was sore, the way she got up and down, but the kid was being very grown up about it. There were a couple of Band-Aids on some of the larger places where her skin had been scraped off, but she had had fun, and to Holly, that was all that really mattered. Merriam, however, was a different matter altogether.

"I should sue those people for what they did to you. Molly, you do know that you're going to be scarred for life now? Just look at you." Molly told her that she'd had fun. "Fun is for poor children. You're wealthy, not some poor fool that can't hold down a job. When your mother dies, you're going to be living with me. And if I don't disown—"

"That's enough." It was the first time that Sawyer had said anything to Merriam since the first day. "Just back off and leave the kid alone. She worked hard for those cuts, and you should be damned proud of her for doing something that she'd never done before. And if you bring up her mother passing again, I will take care that you've got an early grave for yourself."

Molly went and sat on Sawyer's lap. Holly watched the two of them together, their heads close so that they could talk. Holly looked over at Merriam. Her mouth was so pinched that she looked like she'd sucked on an all-day lemon. Roger joined them with a bottle of water for his wife and a glass of tea for her. Sawyer and Molly had declined, as they'd eaten on the way into the hospital. Merriam wasted no time in putting blame where she thought it should be.

"That monster threatened me. I will not allow him to speak to me in such a manner. Take care of him, Roger, by throwing him out of this hospital." Roger turned and looked at Sawyer, who sat Molly on the seat beside him and stood up. Holly hadn't noticed how large Sawyer was until that moment. "Roger, he said that he was going to kill me. What sort of person says that to me? I'm an Addington, for heaven's sake."

"You threaten my wife?" Sawyer said that he had and he'd do it again. Then he told Roger what she'd said to Molly. Roger turned back to his wife. "You actually said that to her? That her mother was going to die? Christ, Merriam, I've put up with a lot from you over the years, but this is the worst yet. That's our daughter, for fuck's sake. Our granddaughter's mother. Why would you say that to them?"

"So you're just going to forget that he threatened me because I said something that we all know is true? Raven has been lingering in that coma for days now, and they're not letting her die so that they can make her bill higher. Why, I'd not—"

"Shut the fuck up about my mom." Holly started for

Molly, thinking that she was too hurt to know what she was saying. "I'm not poor, because my mom works hard for her money. You can shove your money up your butt. My mom is going to live, and if she doesn't, then I'd rather die with her than to step one foot into your house ever again." Merriam drew back to slap her and Molly put her chin out. "Yes, hit me. You go ahead, and I'll never speak to you again. Ever."

The slap nearly knocked her back on her bottom, but it was Sawyer that picked her up and held the sobbing little girl in his arms. When he looked at Roger, Holly was almost afraid of what he was going to say to her son.

"You take her home. I think everyone is a little stressed out and needs a break." Roger nodded, and Merriam said that she wasn't going anywhere, her daughter was hurt. "You get your ass out of here right now before I call the police. You assaulted my stepdaughter, and I'll sue you for every penny you have."

Merriam was still screaming about how Molly had deserved it as Roger dragged her to the elevator. Sawyer held onto Molly, patting her back as he looked at Holly. There was something there—anger, she'd bet, but embarrassment as well.

"I'm sorry that I caused this. I should have held onto my temper better." Holly told him that she was proud of him. "I'm not. I angered Raven's parents, and that's not going to get any of us off on the right foot."

"You're going to mate with Raven then." He said that he really had no choice. "Yes you do, son. She's never met you, and as far as I know, the only time you've seen her is when you were at her side that night."

"I've fallen in love." She asked if it was with Molly. "Yes.

49

My family, they figured out what Raven and Molly were to me. They have already taken her to their hearts just like she's already my daughter."

Molly looked at Sawyer and asked him if that was true, that he was going to have Raven as his mate. He told her that it would be up to her mother.

"Mom will love you as much as I do. And you have a wonderful family." Molly was set back down on the floor, and she went to her grandma. "We picked apples. Bushels and bushels of them. I learned how to ride a bike. I have two new friends that I like. Their momma is dying of cancer, so they can be really sad sometimes. But they come play with me so they can forget about it for a little while."

"Mr. Bishop, you have a phone call." He started toward the nursing station just knowing that he was going to be arrested. It would be his luck to stand up to a bully and be called one himself. Picking up the phone, he said his name.

"Hey, Bishop, it's Jackson from the precinct. We got them. Both of them. You getting that list for us really helped us solve this one. Ms. Addington had fired them both the week before this happened. They'd been jointing it on the job." They'd been smoking pot in other words, Sawyer thought. "Addington has a very strict policy on smoking on the job, and she had caught them twice before this. They didn't want her stinking money, they said, but for her to die. Do you think that the family will press charges too? It would keep them in prison for a good deal longer if they did."

"I'll talk to them about it. Will she need to fill out a statement when she wakes up?" He said that since she'd nearly died and it was revenge, she didn't, but pressing charges would help. "Thanks so much for calling me about this. I'll talk them into it if I have to."

"What are you doing now that you're retired? Are you dating a hundred women a night? You sure did avoid them when you were working all the time. You do know, Bishop, that women love a man in uniform." He laughed with Jackson. "Anything I can do for you, you just let me know, all right?"

"You think you could do me a favor please? If a Mr. Roger Addington or his wife, Merriam, come in or call about me, can you give me a heads up? I'd like to get out of town before I have to be around her again." He asked if it was that bad. "Worse than you can imagine. Ms. Addington is my mate."

Sawyer had to pull the phone from his ear when Jackson whooped it up. After that, they talked about what it was like to have finally found her, and Sawyer only gave short answers. He still didn't know.

"You bring her by sometime and we'll tell her all about her new mate. Christ, you leave the force and find someone to love you. Congratulations, buddy." Sawyer thanked him. "I know that you're there at the hospital. If you get any word about the young lady, let us know. We're rooting for her to come out of this."

After hanging up, he went back to where Holly and Molly were seated and found them gone. The nurse said that they'd gone into visit Ms. Addington. Nodding, he was surprised when she asked him if he wanted to join them. Now that he was semi committed to this, he said that he would.

The room was full of different kinds of machines that were no doubt keeping her alive. When he sat in the corner away from the bed, he watched Molly. Christ, he loved that kid. And his family did as well. Two days with her and they wanted to adopt her themselves.

Molly was telling her mom about her weekend. Talking about learning to ride a bike and how she'd gotten all beaten up over it. "But I know how to ride it now. And Saul is going to pull out one of the bikes in the barn for me. Todd, he's my friend, he said that if they didn't have time, he'd make sure that it was all fixed up for me the next time I came." She looked at him when she paused in the one sided conversation she was having with her mom. "Sippy said that she was taking pictures for me. And when I get a few of them printed from her, I should write what I'd been doing in the picture. Sippy is the best other grandma that I ever had."

Laying her head on the bed, Molly kept talking to her mom about her adventures. Her conversation was getting slower. Her voice was getting quieter too. When she finally gave in to her nap, Sawyer picked her up and laid her gently on the bed next to her mom, very careful of the tubes and other things that were attached to her.

"She is all out in love with your family, Sawyer." He said that they loved her too. "Do you? Are you really thinking of her as your stepdaughter now?"

"No. My daughter. I know that it sounds odd—I know very little about either of them. But I love Molly very much." Holly nodded. "They captured the men. Both of them had been fired the week before they attacked Raven. They'd like for you or your son to come in and press charges. That way things will stick much tighter against them."

"I'll have Brooks take care of it. If I don't let him, he'll be all pissy about me doing things on my own. He's like that about—"

The sound of the monitor had them both standing up. Molly woke up too as they watched the monitor beep like it was racing. Sawyer pulled her off the bed and into his arms. The nursing staff came running in and stood around the bed with the crash cart. Then when it settled out, the sound going back to the simple beep-beep, no one moved when the monitor that had gone off seemed to still.

"Has she ever done that before?" He was so quiet when he asked, and the nurse who told him no was just as quiet. "Does this have to do with her daughter lying next to her?"

"No, oh no. It more than likely made her feel better." The nurse touched her fingers to Molly's cheek. "You did nothing wrong by being next to your momma, honey. I bet she felt you there and woke up a little bit."

Nodding, they all stood around waiting. When it was obvious that nothing more was going to happen, the staff walked out of the room one at a time. Finally Holly sat down, and so did he. Sawyer had never been so terrified in all his life.

Molly did hold her mom's hand, but this time instead of lying next to her, she laid at the foot of the bed and slept. She'd been so excited to come back to her mother today that Sawyer was sure that she'd not slept all that well the night before. Watching the child sleep, knowing that he wasn't going anyplace, he asked Holly if she'd like to take a break and go home for some food and a shower.

"That's an excellent idea. Yes, I've been here now for eight days, and I'm sure that I'm a little smelly. I was going to ask you if you thought that Molly would go with me, but I'm thinking that she's resting just fine where she is." Sawyer told her how excited she'd been to come today. "I've no doubt about that. She sure seemed to have fun. And just look at the tan she's gotten. You took very good care of her, despite what

Merriam said."

"Do you think she's going to be trouble?" Holly just laughed. "Yes, I guess I thought that as well. Roger didn't seem all that happy with her."

"I don't think my son has been happy since the day he married her. Merriam is what I call spoilt. I told Roger he was a fool for marrying her. Then I asked if he loved her. He said that it was better for him to marry her so that she'd stop hounding him about it. I don't think that is a way to start off a marriage, and I do believe that he wishes that he'd listened to me."

"I bet he does too. You go on home and I'll hang around here. Molly has your number, correct?" She asked him if he had it. "I don't have a cell phone. As I'm sure you've figured out, we're a little on the poor side. We don't have it as bad as most do, but we have some financial issues."

"Can I help you out?" Sawyer was embarrassed, and he was sure that she could see it. It was then that he remembered to give her the credit card. She didn't even ask if he'd used it. "Tough guy, huh? Well, if you need me, I'd like to know that you'll call on me. By the way, I wanted to thank your parents for showing Molly such a good time. What are their names?"

"My mom goes by Sippy, but her first name is Serendipity, and my father is Saul. But you don't have to do that, Holly. They were thrilled to have her there. And the neighbor kids were happy to have someone to play with." Holly told him that Molly looked as if she had too. "Molly told my mom that you'd see her cuts as a badge of honor. Her other grandmother not so much."

"Molly won't speak to her, not until she turns things around. One thing I know about my little girl is that she is as stubborn as her momma. And I'm glad for it. There wasn't a single reason for her to slap Molly. That bitch is going to regret this someday." Holly kissed Molly on the forehead and turned to him. "I'll bring us back some dinner. We'll talk more then."

Sawyer watched the women in his life resting. He could only hope that Raven was as accepting as her grandma was. Time would tell, he supposed.

Just as he was settling into his chair, the monitors went off again.

~*~

Holly made a few calls on her way to her home. She had a feeling that she'd be stepping on some toes, but at the moment, she didn't care. Calling Brooks, she told him what she wanted. He laughed and said that he had been thinking of nothing but them since he'd done a search on the family.

"I've made a few more phone calls on your behalf—I hope you don't mind. They're not just broke, Holly—they're very broke. But I've also heard that they are a very giving and a very loving family. There is another family in town that I wish I had known about sooner. Molly knows them. The Littles." She asked if they had two children. "Yes, that's them. The mother only has weeks to live, if that long. They didn't have any insurance, and she was diagnosed with stage four cancer a few months ago. Mr. Little can't hold down a job because he's taking care of his wife and children. And when I say he's taking care of them, I mean the man is a special kind of man."

"The poor man. What can we do to help the family?" Brooks told her funeral expenses. "Set it up for them. But let it be anonymous. I don't want it coming back on Molly that she

55

might have told someone."

"Consider that done. Also, about the Bishops. They have a great many fruit trees and a large garden that they put in every year. They give a great deal of the fruit away to anyone who needs it. Also things from their garden. It's been said that Saul, the father, has been seen plowing fields for someone at no charge. His sons will work their own jobs and go help out at another farm that needs it." Brooks laughed. "Holly, they all send more than half their checks home to their parents to help with bills and such. Sawyer had the best-paying job, but he had to move back home. His father has been pretty weak, I heard."

"That's where he was headed when I asked him to hang out here." Brooks asked her if she knew that the culprits had been caught. "Yes, Sawyer told me before I left. I need for you to go there on Raven's behalf and press charges. I heard that it will be a better sticking point to the two men."

"That's an excellent idea." She told him about the run in with Merriam, and how Roger seemed to have grown some balls. "You're kidding. Christ, I wish I could have been there. What I don't believe that she hit that little girl. There isn't anyone sweeter than Molly."

"Molly has a temper too. You should see her now, Brooks. She's been out in the sun until she's brown. Both her knees and her elbows are like hamburger, but she's proud of them. Learned how to ride a bike, she did. Got herself a black eye, too, from trying to learn now to play baseball." Holly told him about the badge of honor too.

"I'm telling you right now, Holly. The two of them together, Raven and Sawyer, they're going to make a hell—"

"I have a call from Molly. Hang on." After fussing with

the phone a couple of times, she finally got to talk to Sawyer. He was nearly impossible to understand. It wasn't until Holly heard that Raven was awake but groggy that she burst into tears. "I'm on my way back. Oh, my darling is awake."

She nearly forgot about Brooks, but finally got back to him. Telling him that Raven was awake had him cheering too. Having her driver turn around, she told him that she was headed back there now. It was going to be a wonderful ending to this day to see her granddaughter awake for a change.

Holly crept to the room when she heard Molly talking. It must have been to Sawyer, because he was the one that answered her. Holly stood outside the door, listening to his answers to Molly's questions about her mom.

"I know, honey, but she did know who you were, and that's the best kind of sign. She's going to be all right now. You know that, don't you?" Molly must have answered him because Sawyer spoke again. "I know that it's frustrating to have her go back to sleep, but I promise you with all my heart that she's going to be awake longer and longer after this. She's taking a lot of drugs to make sure that she's not hurting. You don't want that, do you?"

"No. She looked right at me and asked me about my eye, didn't she, Sawyer? That means that she knows that I didn't have a black eye before." Sawyer told her that was right. "I was really afraid that she was really going to die like Ms. Addington told me that she was."

"You call her Ms. Addington?" Again, Molly didn't answer loud enough for her to hear. "Molly, if your mom and I can make this work between us, and she doesn't kick me in the head for suggesting we are a couple, if you call my mom Grandma, she'll give you the world. Dad too."

"Can I call them that now? Did you know that Sippy told me that I was her first granddaughter ever? Wesley, he told me that you and my mom were mates, so I know what that means. I'm so happy about that, Sawyer, that I could have a kitten." Sawyer laughed. "You'll make her happy, won't you? My mom, she acts like she's happy, but I don't think she is. I think Ms. Addington wears on her nerves. Ms. Luna told me that once when I was sick. I didn't believe her though. She said it with a grin."

Holly moved into the room then and looked over at her granddaughter. Perhaps it was hopeful thinking, but she thought that Raven looked better. Also, she noticed that a couple of the machines weren't hooked up to her any longer. Sitting in her chair, she looked at Sawyer when he cleared his throat.

"I'd like a connection with you." Holy was confused at first, but before she could tell him that she would be happy for it, he continued. "It'll only be a small bite to your hand. I promise, it won't hurt at all."

"Of course."

She held out her hand and he licked the fatty part where her thumb was connected to her hand. His nip to her skin wasn't painful, and she looked up at him when he closed the wound. It wasn't much, not really, but it must have been enough. He spoke to her then, and she listened intently to his tale.

She died. Right after you left, Raven coded again. This time she didn't wake right away like the last time. I gave her some of my blood. A great deal of it, as a matter of fact, to save her. The nurses took Molly into the hall so that she could not be around while I did it. I didn't want her to freak out about what I had to do. Holly

58

asked what it was he'd done. *I think, because of her wounds, I might have converted her. I can smell a cat on her flesh now.*

I see. She really didn't, but her mind was a kaleidoscope of thoughts. All of it centering on the fact that Raven was going to be really pissed off when she figured this out. *She's a cat, like you. And what does that give her? I'm assuming that she'll heal faster.*

Yes. Not only that, but the wounds that she currently had, they'll all be healed. She's too weak to shift at the moment – that would heal her completely. But she's not going to have any more issues with her dying. Are you upset with me? She just stared at him. *I'm truly sorry that there wasn't time to inform you. But I can't be sorry that I've done this to her. She'll live, and at the time, even now, that was all I could think about. Not just for me, but for Molly as well.*

Well of course you had to do it. I don't even want to think about what I'd have felt if she had died. She did, however, think about what the rest of them would say. He seemed to understand where her mind had gone when he laughed. *Yes, well, you've had one run in with Merriam and came out unscathed. I haven't any idea what she'll do when she finds out that her daughter is a tiger.*

She'll deal with it or not. I won't have her bringing either of them down again. Holly said that she wished him luck with that. *Yes, well, I think I might need it, I'm afraid.*

They sat there for a little while longer. Sawyer answered questions that Molly put to him. Holly listened with half an ear. She was thinking about what would be spewed from Merriam's mouth when she found out about Raven. Merriam had plenty to say when Raven had ended up being a single mom. Holly didn't think this would be any different. Louder and more vicious, yes but nothing would change, and Holly for one was glad that he'd told her first. Now she'd get to see the look on Merriam's face when she found out.

"I'm going to talk to Roger." Sawyer nodded and said nothing more. "Yes, I think I'll have a long talk with my son. I cannot think that after this morning he'd have anything against what you did to save his daughter. Besides, we'll make it so that he has a talk with Merriam when the times comes. I'm very disappointed in him, to say the least."

"Don't be. He's suffered enough with this." Holly knew that he was talking about Raven, but she thought that he'd more than suffered with Merriam all these years. It surprised her daily how the man could have put up with Merriam. "Holly, Raven is awake."

~*~

Raven stared at the man. Her grandmother was speaking to her, but whatever she was saying didn't register in her mind. The man, whoever he was, she felt like she should know him. When Molly stood in front of him, she looked at her daughter and smiled. The man was still in her mind, but her little girl was with her.

"Mommy, are you awake?" Raven didn't know what to say to her, but did nod. "You've woke up several times, but you've never said very much. And that's just not like you. Is your mouth broken?"

"No, I'm just trying to get my bearings. I don't remember how I came to be here. I'm assuming this is the hospital?" Her grandma nodded, wiping at the tears as they flowed down her weathered cheeks. "What happened? Did I have a car accident or something?"

"You were leaving your office and two men jumped you." As the man spoke, all of what had happened came rushing over her, like an electrical storm that was leading up to something more powerful. The man took her hand into his, and she let him. "Breathe, Raven. Just in and out like you do all the time. Breathe in and out."

She did as he said to her. His voice was quiet and calm. Every part of her was in overdrive, like a drag racer about to come to the last lap with hundreds of others trying to vie for her spot. When Raven was able to breathe better, she looked up at him. There was something there, just beyond her reach, and she asked him about it.

"I was the first officer on scene when you called the dispatcher. I'm Sawyer Bishop. I told you about your grandma and your daughter." She nodded, not sure that was all it was that had her wanting him to keep holding onto her like he was. "The men that hurt you, they've been caught and are in jail. You don't have to worry about them again."

"Sawyer." He nodded as he sat across from her. Molly asked if she could lay down with her again, and Sawyer picked her daughter up and put her in the bed with her. "I feel like you've done this before. Watched over me."

"Yes, I've been here since you were brought in. Your grandma asked me to stay in the beginning because of the unknown whereabouts of the perpetrators. Then after that, I found that I couldn't leave you alone." Raven tried to think what that might have meant. No man, so far as she knew, wanted to spend any time with her. Not even long enough for a date to be finished most times. "You're thinking very hard. Just ask me what you're thinking about."

"Why are you still here?" Her face heated up in embarrassment. "What I mean is, after they found the men, why did you hang around? It must have been very boring to be sitting here watching me rest up."

"You'd be surprised. You've been very entertaining to watch when you get up and dance around the room in that gown." Molly laughed, and she told Sawyer that he was being silly. "I fell in love with you and your daughter."

Raven didn't know what to say to that. Surely the man was jesting. Turning to look at her grandma again, she asked her how long she'd been here. When she heard that it had been nine days, she wanted to demand that they tell her the truth. But Grandma assured her that it had been that long.

Sitting up in the bed, she couldn't believe how much better she was feeling with every passing moment. Even holding onto her grandma's hand was a great feeling. Molly laid her head on her breast and Sawyer looked at them. Everything in her body warmed up to the point that she wanted to fan her face. Even to take off the little bit of covers that she had on.

Grandma talked about the things that she'd done for her. Running the company from here. Having her attorney go over and take care of payroll and the such. Even Molly had been taken care of, going to Sawyer's home with his family to get her away from all the things going on here.

"I have to get me something to eat." Grandma stood up and put out her hand to Molly. "Why don't you come with me, child, and I'll get us both something very bad for us in celebration."

"I'd like that."

She wanted to call them back, to beg them not to leave her alone with the man, but they were out the door and no longer her protection. Raven had no idea why she thought that she might need it.

Raven looked at Sawyer again. "I don't know what's

wrong with me. I mean, other than having my body beaten up and waking for the first time in a little over a week." He didn't say anything, and Raven felt her embarrassment turn up, as well as her anger. "Either say something or get the hell out of here."

"I can do that. But you need to know this. You've been coding since you were brought in. Several times on the helicopter, and twice that I know of here in the hospital. The last time you didn't come back to us as quickly, nor as well as they had hoped. So I took measures that saved your life." Raven didn't want to ask him what they were, his measures, but her mouth seemed to be braver than her mind was. She asked him what he'd done. "I'm a Bengal tiger. White. I don't know why we're white. My family has been since the beginning of the line that we've been able to trace back. And in saying that, while you were almost dead this last time, as close as you could come, I gave you a great portion of my blood. In doing so, I believe, but I can't be a hundred percent sure, that I changed you into what I am. A cat."

"You're a shifter." He nodded, and she had to try and get her bearings in the right order. "Who told you that you could do that? I certainly wasn't made aware of it. I doubt that anyone in my family would have been happy about it either. What right did you have to make me into something that I cannot change back?"

"You're my mate. I'm assuming that since you knew that I was called a shifter, you would have to know a little about my kind. You know what a mate is?" She nodded, slowly so as not to jumble all the other thoughts that were in her mind. "Holly knows. She said that she was glad for it, as she didn't know how she'd live without you around. I've not mentioned it to Molly just yet. I didn't know if she'd be able to keep it to herself until your grandma talks to her son. Your mother, she's not happy with me in the first place."

"Did you try and eat her?" Raven had no idea where that thought came from, but she regretted it as soon as it slipped from her mouth. "I'm sorry. I'm confused and feeling off my feet. What happened between you and my mother? I'm assuming that it was entirely her fault. Or did she tell you that you weren't good enough for me because of her being an Addington?"

"Both, actually, but they were neither pointed at me. Not yet at any rate. She's pissed off with your daughter." She asked him over what. "You've seen her. She's banged up. Molly got that playing with the neighborhood children while she was playing at my parents' house." Raven nodded and said nothing more. She didn't know why her mom would think that— "We—my family and I—are very poor, and Merriam pointed out to Molly that children of her stature didn't have fun that was for the poor, then she slapped her."

SAWYER

Chapter 5

Raven thought about all the things that Sawyer had told her. Then, after he'd left—well, she sent him to her home for clothing—she called her grandma. Grandma had a great deal more to say on the subject of the slap than Sawyer had told her.

"You know the stubbornness of Molly, dear. She won't speak to her again. Not until hell freezes over. And did you know that she calls her Ms. Addington? Took me about an hour to figure out that Merriam didn't want her calling her grandma because she wasn't a legitimate Addington." Raven asked her what she'd meant by that. "I went to that club of hers. I wonder if she knows that I have a great many more contacts there than she ever will. Anyway, she told one of her buddies that she didn't count her as her granddaughter because you never married the man. I was so angry that I nearly called her up and gave her a piece of my mind."

So here Raven sat, waiting for her mother to come to the hospital to see her so that she could get to the bottom of a great many things. Sawyer returned with the clothing that her maid had packed up for her and started out the door again.

"Oh no, you don't. Don't you dare leave here without me telling you to." The man was trying her patience, and she wondered if he knew that she was about as close to the edge as she could be right now.

"I can read your mind." She felt her face heat again. Another thing that she was pissed off about with him. "Who shit in your cereal? I wasn't even here. Did your mom call?"

"No, I called her. After I talked to my grandma. Did you know that she's ashamed of Molly?" He nodded, and she could have leapt from the bed and strangled him. When Sawyer laughed, she sat up higher in the bed and calculated the amount of effort it would take to touch him. The low growl from him had her looking away from him. "Don't do that. I don't know if you realize this or not, but it makes me feel weird when you do. I'm not into having a discussion with you regarding that just yet."

"You want me." She started to tell him he was full of shit when he growled low again. "I'm not sure what you want from me when you think of things regarding my body."

"I didn't think of a single thing about your body. Other than your throat. I want to strangle you." Sawyer laughed, and the tingle all over her body came back, like he'd laid a very warm blanket over her. When his body stiffened, she looked him up and down. Sawyer had an erection that made her want to strip him naked and see if he looked as thick and hard as he did with clothing on.

"You keep smelling like that and I'm not going to be held responsible for what happens next."

Licking her lips because there was no moisture in her

body, she shook her head at him, not even sure what she had been telling him about. Her mouth dried up like she'd taken a bite of dust. Raven felt her body warm up to the point of being on fire. His growl this time didn't make her pissed off, but hardened her nipples until they hurt. The pit of her belly was churning. Not from being sick like it usually did, but like she was painfully aware of the man in front of her.

"Hello, darling. I'm so glad that you — What is he doing here? I thought you and I said enough the last time I was here. Go along now, Briar patch boy, and let me talk to my daughter without you interrupting me again." Sawyer didn't take his eyes from Raven's, and Raven wanted to scream at her mom to go the fuck away, they had business. Then her father walked in, and Sawyer sat down on the chair right behind him. "I didn't say to sit, young man. I want you out of here, now. And if you talk to me the way you did before, then I'm going to sue you. See how your poor family likes that."

"Mother, shut the fuck up." Raven was finally able to look away from Sawyer just in time to see her father walk in. "Daddy, I didn't know you were coming in too. Thanks, but I really wanted to talk to Mother alone."

"I'm here in the event that things get out of hand again." Dad's voice was as hard as she'd ever heard it. His anger was dripping off his lips as he spoke too. Raven looked at Sawyer. "Not at him, honey, but your mother. You have no idea what sort of things she spewed at Molly when she was here the last time. Also, she's not talking to her. Your Molly, not your mother. Molly said she wouldn't, and by golly, she's not."

Dad laughed, and Raven felt her anger get harder — her brain hurt with how pissed off she was at her mother. When she started to tell her off, Sawyer scooted his chair next to

67

KATHI S. BARTON

her bed and stretched his legs out in front of him. Raven wasn't sure what that was about, but it didn't cool her temper anymore.

I'm only here in the event that your cat takes control of you. And she will if you don't calm her. Do you feel her, Raven? She's set to protect you. If she gets out, she'll kill your mother. Sawyer told her again to take deep breaths and let them out. *She's your cat, honey. Just tell her that you have this. And she'll believe you. For now. Your mother is upsetting you both, so you need to be in control of yourself. All right?*

When he put his hand near hers on the bed, Raven grabbed it like a lifeline. It was calming for her too, to have him so close. When Sawyer squeezed it, giving her comfort, she thought, Raven realized that her mom was talking to her. Or at her anyway.

"You will not put me through this again, Raven. Do you hear me? You'll not be shacking up with that man there. It's embarrassing to go to the club and have everyone know that you're nothing but a—well, I was going to say whore, but cheap sounds better." Dad tried to get Mother to shut up. "I will not. Someone has to tell her what they're saying about her. And I'm her mother, much as it shames me to say so. You cannot imagine the grief that I've gone through just to say that I have an illegitimate grandchild. My goodness. If he leaves you in that position, I'm going to sue the hell out of all of them. You too while I'm at it, Raven. Don't you think you've hurt me enough with the way you live your life? You should see what they've done to Molly. Her face and hands are scabbed up like she's some ragamuffin. Why can't they just leave us alone and be with their own kind? And her black eye. It's as big as her fist, and she claims that no one hit her.

But Molly has been hanging out with the wrong sort of people, what with her being an Addington."

"Are you finished, Mother?" She said that she was only just getting started. "I see. Well, you have your say, then I'll have mine. You should know that I've been storing up a great deal more than you can imagine. But you go ahead and tell me what it is you have to endure for being my mother."

"I'm glad to see that you're finally going to listen to me, Raven." Mother sat down in the room's other chair and glared at Sawyer. "Did you know that he's an unemployed, broken down police officer? The man that I spoke to told me some wild tales about Mr. Bishop here. That he's been awarded so many awards for his bravery and valor that it made me ill to think that someone would lie like that. He and his family are broke too. That's the only reason that I can think of that he'd be wanting to hang around here with you. I've wondered if his mind was in the right place, but I think he does this because he figures to get some of my money or your grandmother's. She's stupid enough to just hand over her credit cards to him without any qualms about ever getting it back."

"Which is it, Mother? You think that he could do better than to marry someone like me, someone you just called a whore? Or are you upset that he is a good man that might deserve better than me?" Mother huffed at her. "Let me see if I'm getting this straight in my mind. You think that me having Molly has ruined your life at the club. That everyone is talking about you because of me. Oh, and let's not forget about me being stupid and just simply handing over my money to someone I've only just met about an hour ago."

"You have it about right. I swear, I don't know how this family kept their good name intact before I came around. Just the other day, I heard your father talking out on the front lawn. He had his arm around the kid that delivers our papers like he was some buddy that he'd met up with at the club." Mother huffed again. "I had to have the kid taken off our route so that your father wouldn't embarrass me like that again."

"You make him bring the paper up to the front door and hand it to the butler, Merriam. Do you have any idea how that might affect him? How much longer it takes him to do that when he has baseball practice and homework?" Raven looked at her dad, feeling sorry for him for the first time in her life. Dad continued, his voice hard but low. "You had him fired, not put on a different route, Merriam. Fired. All he was trying to do was help out his family as they put their oldest through college."

"So? I don't care what he's telling you—it's more than likely a lie anyway—but I want the paper handed to me. It's the least he can do for what he charges me every month." He asked her what the bill was, and Raven watched her mother. "I don't know, Roger. I have nothing to do with that sort of thing. I just know that you're paying too much for him to bring it to us. Why, you own the paper anyway. Why are we even paying someone to deliver it when the entire company owes us a great deal?"

"It doesn't matter to you, does it, that I had to bring that young man into my offices and explain to him why you were such a bitch. And I did too." Merriam looked like she could kill him right then, Raven saw. "He's a good kid, and working out very well in delivering the mail to the offices in my building. So thank you for that find."

"So, Mother, you're not only a bitch to your own family, but to others as well." Raven felt Sawyer squeeze her hand a little bit tighter, and she let out breaths again. When she was calm enough to speak, Raven asked her mother what she'd been burning to ask her all morning. "Why did you slap my child?"

"I didn't hurt her. Is that what they told you? You'd think that she actually fallen to the floor when she did nothing more than take a step back." Sawyer said that he'd caught Molly before she hit the floor. "Everyone is making this out to be more than it really is. It was nothing, I tell you. And to be honest with you, Raven, I wish that I had done it more to you when you were a child. Perhaps then you'd not have brought so much grief down on our heads when you scandalized this family and the Addington name."

Raven had so much more that she wanted to say. A great deal more about being a grandmother and how her own would have handled it. When Sawyer asked her if she was all right, she nodded. Then picking up the phone that was beside her, she made a call to her attorney.

"Hello, Johnson. This is Raven Addington." She told him that she was getting much better and feeling like she could come back to work soon. Mother said that she was not, and Dad just sat there. He looked broken. "I need for you to do a few things for me, but I'd like it if you could come here to get them started. Anytime that's good for you."

"I can come there in about an hour if that's all right with you." She said it would be perfect. "Anything that I can do from here now, Raven? You know that I'd do just about anything for you."

"No. When you arrive I'll be ready with everything that I want lined up. There is a great deal of it too, Johnson, so you might want to hire on some other workers. I, of course, will take care of the extra pay for you." Mother said that she would not be paying anything extra. Raven told her to shut up again. "Also, could you please bring me in a few things from my office? I'll have Mary have them ready for you." After ringing off with him, she looked at her mother.

"What do you plan to do, Raven? Give away all your money? I won't allow you to do that. I'll be right there when Mr. Boggs arrives to tell him what he can and can't do." Raven told her mother that she was twenty-nine years old and Merriam looked around. "Hush. Do you want people to hear you? My goodness, Raven, you don't give away your age like it's something that everyone should be aware of. Why, if you do that, then they'll figure out that I'm much older than I tell people I am."

"Get out." Mother looked at Sawyer when she told her that. "No, Mother, I want you out of my room right now. And if you think that I've embarrassed you at the club, whatever will you do if they find out that I had you arrested for trespassing where you were no longer needed?"

"You have no right to do this to me. It's all him, isn't it? You're trying your best to make me feel bad for telling you the truth. Well, Raven Holly Addington, I will not allow you to make me the bad guy in your life." Raven stood up and watched her mother's face pale. "You're well."

"You're damned right that I'm well. And if you do not leave my room this moment, I will hurt you. Get out, and do not return until I tell you to." Mother stood up, and Dad did as well. "Also, Mother, if you ever touch my child again, you will never have to worry about how we've embarrassed you. You'll never see us or hear from either of us again."

"I'm leaving, but only because I feel that you need to cool

off. You will treat me with the respect that I deserve as your mother." Raven said that she was getting more respect from her than she deserved. "I'm leaving. Not because you told me to, but because I feel that you need to calm down and think about what you're saying."

Merriam turned to the door, and Raven's dad came back and kissed her on the forehead. He told her that he was sorry and that he'd keep Mom away. He would, too, even if he had to fire every person that worked for him. Mother would never stoop to taking a cab anywhere, Raven thought.

Sawyer stood up, his body close to her bed. When he stretched his arms over his head, Raven had to remind herself to breathe again. He said that he was going home, as she'd be busy.

"No, I want you to stay. When my attorney arrives, you and I are getting married. Today, if he can make it happen."

~*~

Sawyer drove home with a heavy heart. He and Raven had had their first fight, and it had been a huge one. He wasn't going to marry her to make her mom more pissed off. And he certainly wasn't going to marry her without making sure she understood what marrying him meant. For her at least. He was coming into this—whatever it was—with his eyes wide open. She didn't know shit about him or his financial standing. Which was pretty much zero right now.

He'd thought to have a job by now, at the very least to have put in some applications. But all he'd been able to do was stay with Molly and Raven through the week and help out around the farm on the weekends. Soon the latter of the two of his jobs would be put away for winter. Not that they stopped working on things, but it would be less stressful between getting the crops in and clearing the fields for next year's growing season.

What's going on? He asked his dad what he meant. *I just had a phone call from Merriam Addington, and she told me that I was beneath her and that you and Raven were not getting married.*

She's right, don't you think? Dad blustered about how they were good enough for anyone. *I'm sure you're right, but we are beneath them when it comes to money. Anyway, I'm not going to marry Raven just because she wants to get back at her mother. That's what she wants to do.*

I see. No one told me about that. He drove for another mile or so before his dad spoke again. *Molly, I'm sure going to miss that little girl not coming around too much. She's a sweet little thing when you compare her to her grandma Addington.*

That's what she calls her, Ms. Addington instead of Grandma. Molly is biting at the bit to call you and Mom her grandda and grandma. She loves you as much as I do. Dad said that would be nice. *I don't know what to do about any of this. While I'd like to marry Raven, I don't want to do it this way. It's just doesn't seem right.*

Let me ask you something, son. And this is just me asking, not trying to talk you into anything. But would it be so bad marrying her for whatever reason that you can? I mean, you said yourself that you're nearly there anyway. I also have a feeling that Molly is going to need some protecting before this is all said and done. Regardless of how the wedding takes place. He didn't answer his dad, not sure yet where he was going. *You marrying this woman, is it going to mean a hill of beans why the two of you wed so long as you're married when the crap hits the fan? After talking to that other woman, I have a feeling that it's going to regardless of your wedded status.*

She doesn't know everything about us. Dad told him that would be settled after the dust was done moving. *What if you don't like her?*

Son, I don't know if you realize this or not, but somebody with a good heart sure did raise that little girl up right. Don't you think? He said that was true. *You do what you want. But I'm thinking that you saving her butt will be a sight better than her taking a tumble and getting badly hurt while you're here at the ranch.*

I guess you're right. I don't know, however, if the wedding is still on or not, to tell you the truth. We parted terms very badly. Dad laughed. *You think this is funny?*

Sawyer, I'm thinking that the fire in the two of you could be just the ticket to shake things up a bit around here. He grinned at what his dad said. *You get in touch with that bride of yours, and I'll get your mom to get us a wedding here all set up. That is, if we don't embarrass you none to be having it here.*

I'm never embarrassed about you or where I come from. She might be, but I suppose that is the point, isn't it? To show her just what we are. Dad said there was that too. *All right. I'll go and talk to her. She might still be pissed at me, just so you know.*

I think we can figure out something about that. Don't you think? Sawyer took the next turn off and got back on the highway. *Sawyer, a big limo just pulled up in front of the house. I'm thinking that it's your in-laws. You best be coming here first.*

Sawyer did another turn and was headed back to his parents' home. He didn't hear anymore from his father, and that made him nervous too. Sawyer wasn't sure if they'd all be fighting in the front yard when he got there, or if he was going to be walking into a bloodied mess of bodies and cats.

By the time he got home, he was a mess of worry. Pulling in behind the limo, he was afraid to go into the house. When he got out, he was greeted by the best hug he'd had all day. Molly was back, and she was talking a mile a minute about so many things that he had to slow her down to make sense of it all.

Before Molly could repeat what she'd been saying, Holly and Raven came out onto the front porch. Holly was grinning from ear to ear, and Raven looked like she could bite a ten penny nail in two and not bust her teeth.

"Hello, Sawyer. My, what a lovely place you have here. I've not been on a farm since I was a small child. This is a beautifully maintained place. I hope you're proud of it." He said that he was, and of his family. "Of course you are. They're wonderful people. That being said, I'm going to take little Molly here inside and have another piece of pie. My goodness, your mother sure can cook."

He moved to the porch, but didn't step up the two steps to be standing with Raven. She had her arms over her breasts and her foot was tapping a mile a minute. He looked at her, from her head to her tapping foot, before he looked at her face.

"I've never seen you standing up before. You're much taller than I thought you were." Her foot tapped harder and faster. "You're going to wear a hole in those pretty shoes if you don't stop that and tell me what has you all fired up."

"You have me all fired up, you moron. What did you think you were doing when you walked out on me right in the middle of an argument?" He took one of the steps up, liking the way her cheeks pinked up when she was yelling at him. "I still had plenty to say to you, and you just left me there. I won't put up with that."

"You sure do have a lot of rules for me when I've not

agreed to marrying you yet." She backed up when he took the next step up. Sawyer realized that he was a step taller than her. The way they were standing now, him on one step below her, made her mouth just where he could kiss her. "Your mom called my dad and told him that we were beneath her. That didn't set too well with me. She also told him that we were not marrying."

"My mother doesn't think I'm worthy either, so we should get along pretty good on that corner, don't you think?" He stood on the same level she was on. "I have us a license and everything is filled out. I'm to understand that your father knows a few people that could come out here and marry us right now."

"Why the rush?" He moved her hair back from her cheek and then ran his fingers down her cheek to her lips. "You're very beautiful when you're pissed, did you know that? I think you're beautiful all the time, but out of the bed and looking like you are, I could take you against that wall behind you and give us both a great deal of pleasure."

"Are you saying that I couldn't give you pleasure, Sawyer?" Her voice was husky, her breaths hot as she spoke to him. "Will you kiss me? I have a feeling that you will make me feel like no one has before."

"You know nothing about me, Raven. You don't have any idea how we're struggling here every day that—"

Raven pulled him to her body, her mouth making short work of tasting him. When she lifted her head, the kiss entirely too short for him, she looked into his face and he could see her cat just on the surface.

"I know a great deal about you, Sawyer. You come from a long line of white tigers. Your family is one of the most generous families in the entire state. Even at the risk of not getting your own crops in, you will help out someone that needs it." He said that was just people talking. "Perhaps. You're also in debt up to your forehead. So are your brothers and parents. There is a lien against their home that is more than can be met with the money that is coming in. Your parents took out a second mortgage on this farm to help pay for the funeral for your grandparents when they were killed a few years ago. Even though your father has several brothers and sisters that could have easily helped out, they refused to do so because they were left nothing in the will. Even the money that your father was left, he used it to pay off yours and your brothers' educations instead of paying down the mortgage. That is where they got into the most trouble, isn't it?"

"For the most part. Then my dad got sick—not unusual at his age—but he didn't recover fast enough for him to get his crops out, and then when it came to reaping his harvest, it isn't going to be enough to feed us this winter. I have to get a job." He looked at her mouth, and his cock hardened when she licked her lips. "I want to taste you, Raven. But when I do, I want you to understand that it will bind us in ways that will make us a couple no matter what I say to the contrary."

"Please, Sawyer, kiss me." He leaned in closer, feeling the warmth of her breath again. Her scent, strong and full of need, made him groan. "Please."

He didn't want to overwhelm her; his need was much stronger than hers. But tasting her again, feeling her lips open under his own, made him dizzy with anticipation, to have her beneath him, to taste parts of her that seemed to call to him. Sawyer pulled her bottom to him, letting her feel him and his hardness. Lifting his head when he could hear someone coming, he held her to him so as to hide his erection from his mother.

"The minister has arrived. Are you ready for this?"

Raven looked at him and he nodded at her, then asked if she was sure.

"As sure as I have been of any decision in my life. The only thing I ask is, don't let my mother run over you." He said that he wouldn't allow her to run over her either. "Just keep Molly safe. Please."

"Yes, forever. Both of you."

He kissed her again and they went into the house. They'd either be happy after today, or regretting this for a very long time.

Chapter 6

It had been a wedding to remember, Raven thought. She was dressed in a borrowed dress from his mom, and Sawyer had on a pair of dark jeans and a plaid shirt. Even her ring that he put on her finger was borrowed. Her grandma gave her the rings that she'd carried around her neck on a gold chain since Grandda had passed away. They both, his and hers, fit like they'd been made for them.

Sippy put on a huge feast. It was nothing like she would have chosen for a big day like this, but it was the most delicious food Raven had ever eaten. Corn bread and fresh green beans, freshly sliced tomatoes, as well as corn on the cob. And for their wedding dessert, there was peach cobbler, apple pies, and cherry Brown Betty. Raven tried a little of everything.

Her dad had told Mom that he was going out of town for a couple of days. Instead, he'd been there to give her away. He, too, was dressed in jeans and a shirt. Dad even got to wear his cowboy boots that had been gathering dust in his closet, he told them, for the last few years. Dad looked amazing.

"Thanks for not turning your nose up at this feast." She looked at her new father-in-law and asked him what he meant. "I know that this isn't up to your usual standard, but we do the best we can."

"I love this, Saul. Every morsel of it." She kissed him on his cheek. "I'm so glad that you did this for us. It's probably the most festive wedding I have ever attended. And I'm happy, now that I've met you, to be a part of this family."

"You're a good girl. That daughter of yours, she could have only been raised by a caring and wonderful person. I've fallen in love with the two of you." She kissed him again, and took his hand into hers. "You gonna tell me that you were just kidding?"

"No. But you have given me an idea where Sawyer gets his lack of optimism. I'm having a wonderful time. I do need to talk to you all for a bit. It's something that my grandma did for me." He asked her what it was, to tell him straight up. "I paid off your home and the back taxes. There is money in your accounts to pay off all your bills, including any medical bills."

"You shouldn't have done that, Raven. We're getting by all right." She just watched his face. "Raven, honey, I don't want you thinking that you have to bail us out when we get a little behind. It's not right."

"It's very right, as far as I'm concerned. You're good people, and I'm glad to be a part of this family. And there is no reason whatsoever that you have to do without just because you got sick, Saul." He nodded, and told her that he'd pay her back. "You want to pay me back? Then I'd like for you to make sure that my daughter is loved like a grandparent should love her. Take her on more adventures with you than she's ever been on so far. When you meet my mother, and I have no doubt that you will, you'll see why it's so very important to me to have Molly know that there are very good people in the world that can and will love her."

"We sure do love her. And I've a feeling that we'll be loving you more than we are right now too. But don't tell Sawyer's mom just yet. She'll get herself in a tizzy about it, and that will spoil your day."

Someone knocked on the door and Saul excused himself to go answer it. As soon as he was at the door, Raven knew who had come to their wedding.

"Mother. You weren't invited here." Merriam huffed at her and grabbed her arm. The room went so silent that Raven was sure that there could have been a shot fired two miles away and they'd have heard it. "Let me go or I will hurt you."

"You will not marry this man. I cannot believe that you'd even consider it after what I told you. They're nothing to us. Nothing at all. Come on, before it's too late." Raven could feel Sawyer coming up behind her before she felt his arm around her waist. "What? Are you going to have me arrested for coming to my only child's rescue? I'm an Addington, and so is my daughter. Either unhand her or so help me, I'll have you living in a cardboard box rather than this piece of crap falling down house."

"Raven and I were married an hour ago. We were just having our dessert when you blew in. It was a lovely wedding too, in the event that you're interested." Mother said that she was not. "Well, suit yourself. Once we have the paperwork ready, I'm going to adopt Molly too."

"Can I call you Daddy then?" Raven hadn't seen Molly until she spoke. She didn't turn to greet her grandmother, and that was very telling. Molly was without a doubt polite to everyone. But Mother had hurt her. "I'm going to have the best grandma and grandpas in the world too. Grandpa Saul is going to teach me to fish—"

"You will not call them your grandparents, young lady. Do not make me have to teach you a lesson again." Molly buried her face in Sawyer's leg, but didn't turn to her grandmother. "Come here this minute. I will not have you acting like a witless fool over this. Molly Anne, I am not joking here. Come to me this very moment."

"I haven't any idea what kind of lessons you've been giving my daughter, Ms. Addington, but you touch her again and I will rip you to shreds."

Raven's dad came up to stand by Molly and took her hand in his. Raven was glad that she went with him willingly.

"Roger, what are you—? You lied to me. You came here to this travesty of a wedding and lied to me. I'll never forgive you for this." Dad handed Molly off to Sippy, who was standing close to them. Mother decided to lay down the law to Dad, and Raven was glad that Molly wouldn't hear it. "You're to come home with me this minute. If I had known that you would lower yourself to lying to me over this, I would not have allowed you to leave. The nerve of you, coming here and not telling me about it."

"You would have raised a ruckus, and I didn't feel like hearing it. And as to you telling me what I was going to do, I'll have you know that I was running a multi-billion dollar company long before you came along." Dad stood beside Sawyer. "I like this man. He's solid and has a good family behind him. His family has done nothing but be nice to me, despite you being a royal bitch about this. I'm glad that they got married. I couldn't have picked a better man for my little girl to be married to. As for Molly, you hurt her again and I will leave you for good. I'm serious about this, Merriam. And you're to leave Raven and Sawyer here alone, too. They don't need your acidy tone and bad manners bringing them down."

Whatever Raven expected from her mother wasn't for her to punch her in the face. It didn't hurt much, but it did startle her enough to have her falling back onto Sawyer and them both hitting the floor. Raven held onto her cat with the help of Sawyer again. When she was calmer, both her and her cat, he stood up.

"You fucking bitch."

That was all the further Sawyer got before Dad stood in front of him. It was going to be bad, she knew it, and stood up with the help of Chandler, one of Sawyer's brothers. She didn't touch Sawyer because she could feel his cat. It was like a very large monster just on the edge of being released. Raven was glad that her dad stepped in.

"Get out of here right now." He turned to her attorney and glared at him. "You go with her and put her in a hotel or something around here. When you do that, you let me know. I have a few things to take care of myself."

"Yes sir."

Raven was surprised when her mother left without a word. Usually this was where she started screaming about how she'd done nothing wrong. That she was an Addington and above people getting pissed at her.

As she was led out the door, Dad turned to her and Sawyer. "I'm working on keeping my temper under control here, so if I sound pissed at you, I don't want you to take it that way." Sawyer nodded and pulled her into his arms.

"I'm glad to have you a part of his family, despite what my wife said. And if you'd be so kind as to come to my offices on Monday, I'd very much like to talk to you about a few things there as well."

"Sir, this is only Saturday. If you don't mind, I'd like to wait until at least Wednesday." Dad looked confused, then nodded after his face turned a nice shade of red. "Thank you, sir. And thank you for having your wife escorted out."

"Well, I don't know how she found out, but you can bet your ass that I'll take care of that person too." Dad shook himself as if he needed to shake off the anger that he had. "I'm sorry, son, I truly am, that she came here and did this to you both."

"It's fine, sir. I have to tell you something about her attacking Raven. You know what I am. What you don't know is that in order to save her, I gave her some of my blood." Roger nodded, and said that he'd figured that out when Merriam attacked Raven. "I'm not going to tell you that I'm sorry. It was her life that I was saving."

"Never apologize to me about keeping my family safe, Sawyer. I don't know why this is, but I trust you over all the men that work in security for me." He looked at the door again, and then Dad turned back to her. "I love you, Raven. So much that it hurts me the way that your own mother has treated you. I wish that I could take Molly home with me for the next few days, but I have a feeling that I need to shelter her away from what is about to happen."

"You're going to divorce her, aren't you?" Grandma came to Dad's side as she asked him what he was about to do. "It'll be hard on you, Roger, but I think that in the long run, you might be able to have a life that you've not been able to have before this. Good luck. And if you need me, you just call. I can have Brooks go along with you if you need him to. He's been known to hustle things along when they're needed."

"I'd appreciate that, Mom. I'm sorry about this. I should have listened to you." Grandma hugged Dad, then kissed him on the cheek. "You're the best mom a man in trouble with his wife could ask for."

"Change the locks as soon as you can, sir." Dad looked at Sawyer and asked if there was more he could do. "Yes, sir. If the bank accounts are in both your names, I'd drain them into one she can't get to. Cancel all cards, and make sure that you have a guard that you can trust at any of your businesses. I don't suppose you have a pre nup, do you?"

"I do, as a matter of fact. All the business accounts are in my name. The checking account that we use to pay bills is only in my attorney's name. Credit cards will be cut off as soon as I get into my car." Sawyer told him to not allow anyone to pay his bills but him. That way he could have a better handle on his worth. "Thank you. I've known about that little tidbit for a while, but never got around to changing it. I think having you as a son-in-law will help me a great deal."

After Dad left, Raven turned in Sawyer's arms and looked up at him. He was a handsome man, and she sort of liked him. She smiled at him, and Sawyer asked her what she was thinking.

"I thought you could read my mind." He told her that he didn't do it unless it was necessary. "I think this would be considered necessary, don't you?"

"Are you trying to seduce me, Mrs. Bishop?" Nodding at him, Raven thought of all the most erotic things she'd ever read in books. She knew the moment that he dove into her thoughts and saw what she'd been thinking of. "You keep this up and we'll never make it to pictures."

"Do we need a reminder of this day, Sawyer?" He picked her up off the floor just enough to have his body press against hers, groin to pussy, his hard cock so yummy feeling against her. Her breasts ached to have him touch them, make them his. "You're going to make me come if you keep this up. And I want you to know that I'm a screamer."

"Good. I plan on making you hoarse for the next several days. And forever after that."

They stood for several pictures, but didn't stop touching each other. Raven didn't know where they were going to spend their honeymoon, but she hoped it was someplace with padded walls. Because for all his saying that he was going to make her scream, she planned to do the same to him.

~*~

Holly helped with the cleanup. She was thrilled that Sawyer had allowed her to pay for a hotel room for them. If they made it that far, she thought with a giggle. Holly was sure that the two of them were in love, but neither of them had realized it as yet. She was going to love having that young man around, she knew it.

"I'm sorry about your son and his wife." She looked at one of Sawyer's brothers and couldn't remember his name. He handed her the next plate that she was to dry after he washed it, and grinned at her. "I'm Dwayne. Second from the youngest. Your son, he has his hands full, I think. That wife is a real treat, isn't she?"

"She's a bitch, if you don't mind me saying so." They both laughed. "You and your brothers, you do a good job here taking care of your parents. I'm so glad that I got to meet

87

them."

"They really didn't want to do this, have you guys over. Mom isn't a proud person, but you have money and we don't." Holly asked if that bothered him. "I don't know. I've never known anyone that had a great deal of money. Or if you're asking me if it bothers me that we don't have money, then I'd have to tell you that I think we might be richer than you on some things. Since we were kids, my parents have taught us to take care of each other and those that needed us. We have a great many friends here. Most of them have broken bread with us until they were able to find a way to feed themselves. My dad, he works hard, and most of the time there isn't any meat on the table. But it's good solid food that warms not just our bellies, but our hearts too."

"What is it you do, Dwayne? I know that your brother Gunner isn't here because he's out on duty. Chandler there, he's good with animals and had a desire to go to college to be a farm vet. Wesley, he works here, and that's about all I could get from him. Quincy — well, it took Raven asking him point blank what he did for a living to get it out of him. He works at the local hospital in the nursery, caring for babies when they have no one else. Quincy would make a great doctor, don't you think?"

"He would. It's a dream of his." Holly watched as Dwayne washed up two more dishes and set them in the drainer. "All of us have had dreams of making it big. Not in a flashy sort of way, but a way that could keep my parents in this home and us in pocket money. I had a chance at being able to go to college on a football scholarship, but I guess you could say that life got in the way. I fell off the tractor bed while loading hay on it, and busted my knee all to pieces. After that, all sorts of dreams came to an end. I've been working at the grocery store since then, ringing people out and bagging things up. It's not the football career that I wanted, but it makes me feel good about myself when I get someone to smile at me. We all have a college education. Just the basic stuff for each of us. Sawyer is the only one that went to night school to better himself. It was hard, but he made it work."

"You were helping someone out, weren't you? Gathering up hay or baling it for a neighbor that needed your help." He didn't say anything, but the look on his face was enough. "I've a job for you, Dwayne."

"Mrs. Addington, you don't have to treat us like little puppies that you've found on the side of the road. I'm happy for my brother. Not the least bit envious of him and his good luck at finding himself a mate. Well, perhaps the mate part, but not his future. The rest of us will be there someday." She hugged him to him. "Thank you for that."

"Now, young man. There are a few things that you're going to learn about me. First of all, I never do a damned thing that I don't want to. Including giving you a job. Secondly, I'm not one to beat around the bush on things. I'll tell you like it is if I think you need it. I expect the same thing from you." He grinned, and she was both charmed and happy with the boy. "You'll come to my office on Monday afternoon. No, that won't work. I have a meeting with several of my business heads for.... I'll tell you what, Dwayne, I'll send a car for you Monday morning. Is seven too early?"

"No ma'am, I live on a farm. We're up at the butt crack of dawn, as my grandda used to say." She smiled back at him, and they talked about all sorts of things while they finished up. When he was finished with the dishes, Dwayne took out the trash without being asked or told, put a load of laundry in the washer, then swept the floor, all the while talking to her about cows and such. Holly couldn't wait to see this man in a three piece suit talking to businessmen that might need a helping hand once in a while.

After the dishes were cleaned up, she walked into the dining room. This was, she thought, the heart of the home. When she'd shown up today, they were making the wedding feast and talking and joking around. Even telling them what she knew about Sawyer, Holly noticed that they all looked her in the eyes, and didn't say anything other than to convey politeness and good manners.

Holly wasn't impressed by people that thought that they were beneath her, or even above her in status. She didn't care for the classes that people would feel they were put in, no more than she liked it when people turned their nose up at someone that wasn't as wealthy as they were. Holly knew most of the people that came to work in her offices, and had taken great measures to make sure that she knew birthdays and anniversary dates when they started working for her. It's what she expected from those with people working under them, too.

Everyone at her businesses made a difference to the company, and she had better never hear of someone taking advantage of others working or she'd take care of them right now. That policy was one that she made sure everyone in her business followed, no matter if they were vice president or the man that mopped up the floors. Employees were to be treated like the higher-ups wanted to be treated.

Sitting in the living room of her home around midnight— Holly had always been a late nighter on the weekends—she realized how lonely she was all of a sudden. There weren't any cows mooing around her home, no conversations that would have her smiling or even laughing out loud. She even missed the tea that had been brewed for her that had been the cheapest box, because that was all the Bishops could afford.

Her phone ringing took her out of the need to drive back to their home.

"I have to tell you, Holly, I've never seen Roger so happy before." Brooks never started a conversation out with something so mundane as hello or are you busy. He, like her, got right to the heart of things. "The locks have been all changed, and he did just what Sawyer told him and drained the accounts that they had. I'm not sure that we could have planned this entire thing out without the help of young Sawyer."

"He does seem to have a good head on his shoulders. What happened when he confronted Merriam? I'm sure that it didn't go well." Brooks laughed and said that it had yet to happen. "You're not telling me that he's backed out of this, are you? I swear I never beat him enough as a child. What's he saying now?"

"He's going through with it, I promise you. But he's had her put in a hotel along the route into town. A smallish one that has barely a rating anywhere. Clean and efficient was what it said, and she's already calling him, bitching about how she is an Addington. You'd think that she was the first one of you guys rather than just someone that married an Addington. To be truthful, Holly, I've never cared for her. Not ever."

"Me either. What else has Roger done? I'm sure that I'm going to love every minute of it. I'll have to be at his house when he talks to Merriam." Brooks told her that it was going to be at the hotel. "Even better. I love it. Perhaps I can purchase the hotel, and then have them record the meeting from every angle. That would be something that I'd play on the big screen and watch over and over again. What do you think, Brooks?"

"I think that you should just stay away and let me do the recording for you." Holly pouted, and realized that Brooks couldn't see her. "They're meeting at ten. I'm to understand that you've hired one of the Bishop boys. Which one, and what will he be doing for you?"

"I did hire one. Dwayne. If this works out the way I think it will, I might just hire the whole lot of them. I've been around for a long time, Brooks, and I've never met a family so dedicated to each other in my life. And kind to those that need them." He agreed with her. "Dwayne is going to be my reasonable mind. I think once he understands what it is I do, he'll be the strong arm that makes the men that I'm trying to buy out realize that I only have theirs and the rest of the world's best interest at heart. Not that they don't know that now, but I'm going to need someone to help me in my golden years. And I think he's just the man."

"I agree with you on that. And as for golden years, I think—" Holly reminded him that he worked for her. "Yes I do. And never has a man enjoyed a job as much as I do. Also, Roger hired Sawyer. He's going to teach him the business for the same reasons that you are Dwayne. I think Roger has been waiting for someone to come along for a while now that he could mold into his image. Sawyer might be a better man than Roger is, if I don't miss the clues from them."

"What do you think that Raven will say, if Roger takes Sawyer over her? I mean, she does have her own money-making business, but her daddy is a great man, now that

SAWYER

he's gotten his head out of his ass." Brooks laughed, and then told her that he didn't foresee anything coming between the couple. "I surely hope not. But I have to tell you, I'm betting that Merriam won't go quietly into the night. She's going to be coming back on them, blaming them for Roger getting his act together."

"I'm sure of it. And so is Roger. He told me on the way to his house that he thought that Sawyer could handle himself, but he was more worried about Molly. He thinks she'll be hurt the worst if Merriam interferes in their lives more than she has before." Holly asked him what he thought Sawyer would do if that happened. "He'll kill her. There is no doubt in my mind that he'll protect Raven and Molly with his life."

"I hope you're right."

After hanging up with Brooks, promising him once again that she'd stay at her offices, she thought of the list she needed to make up of things she wanted Dwayne to be able to do at her first meeting. Then she tossed it away. Dwayne needed to be passionate about what he said, and having a script would not allow that. She'd not throw him to the wolves, so to speak, but she would keep an eye on him when things got out of hand.

Holly had been trying to broker a deal with Sampson and Sons for three months, and this was her first meeting with him. Sampson would play ball with her or she'd have to take him to court. Loaning someone money to bring their company up to standard did not mean that they could use that money to go on lavish cruises or long vacations. He'd pay her back or she'd own his ass. And his home, his cars, and the new boat he'd gotten just last week.

"Fool. He thinks that putting the things he got into his

93

son's name would throw me off. I have news for him—I'm a great deal smarter than he'll ever be."

Making her way up to her bed, her cell phone went off. It was Merriam.

"What is it? I'm off to bed, Merriam." She told her what her son had done to her, as if she'd not been there with him. "If you're looking for me to bail you out of the mess you made, you're far stupider than I first thought you were. You made your bed, Merriam, so you deal with it."

"He thinks he's going to divorce me. Holly, I'm an Addington. Addington's do not throw their wives aside like nothing. I've given him thirty years of my life." Holly told her that she'd given him thirty years of hateful words and meanness. "I have not. I swear, there are times that I wish that I'd poisoned you. You're the meanest woman I know."

"You just threatened me, Merriam. What do you think the courts are going to say about that?" Merriam screamed into the phone, making it so that Holly had to pull the phone back from her ear. When she finished, Holly was laughing as she continued. "You are aware that this phone call is being recorded, aren't you? I mean, it says it about three times before you get connected to my life."

"Oh, go to hell, you old bag."

Holly was still laughing as she made her way up the rest of the stairs. Boy, was Merriam going to pay for that little outburst. Laughing harder, Holly forwarded the voice message to her son and got into bed. Tomorrow was going to be the beginning of a whole new day, and she was going to enjoy it more than any she'd had since her husband passed away. Kissing his picture that had been at her bedside since they'd been wed, she laid back down and smiled. Closing her eyes, she let sleep take her.

Holly thought that she might be having more fun than anyone with this divorce. She might even enjoy the hearing too, if it came to that. Her son had never made her more proud than she was of him right now.

Chapter 7

The hotel was nicer than he'd ever been in before. Of course, this was only the second time he'd been in one, but he had a feeling that this one was the best there was. Picking up the champagne bottle that was on ice, he read the label before putting it back in the coldness of the icy container.

There was a basket of fruit too—from the hotel, it said on the label, for their wedding bliss. He wanted to take an apple or two to eat—he'd not eaten enough at home earlier—but he didn't know what to do to get the basket uncovered. He thought of ripping the plastic off it, but he wanted Raven to pick out what she wanted before he destroyed it.

"Are you nervous?" He turned to look at Raven, who had been sitting on the edge of the bed. "I am, if that helps. I've never been married, but I have a child. It hadn't occurred to me that you might not want to have a ready-made family."

"I love Molly and the rest of your family." He thought about telling her that he loved her too, but he wasn't sure that she could handle that so quickly in this relationship. Raven asked him if that meant her mom, if he loved her too. "She might not be one to love me back, but I respect her for having a daughter that I could marry. Why are you nervous? Are you afraid of me?"

"No. I don't have any idea why, but I'm not afraid of you. Nor anyone in your family, as a matter of fact." He sat down next to her on the bed. Sawyer asked her how she felt about being a cat. "I'm not sure on that one either. I'm glad that you saved my life. I'd hate to leave Molly alone. My grandmother wouldn't have survived having someone taken from her again. She lost it big time when Grandda died. I think that Molly is the only thing that kept her from joining him."

"That's the way our kind is. When a mate dies, no matter how, it is hard on them. They only want to join them in the afterlife. I'm not sure that I believe in the hereafter, not like they do, but I do believe that there is a higher power that keeps us going for one reason or another." She smiled at him. "I guess I am nervous. I'm a large man, and you're so delicate. I could easily break some part of you and not mean it." Raven pushed him back on the bed and sat across his lap. "You're very aggressive, aren't you?"

"I go after what I want." Raven unbuttoned his shirt, then kissed his chest. He could feel his cock stretching beneath her, and wanted to flip her to her back and take her, but she was having so much fun he wanted to let her have her way with him. "You're just going to let me do this to you?"

"Yes, so long as you realize that I get to have my way with you too." She seemed to think on it a little while, but he wasn't worried. Either she had her fill of him, or he'd take his fill from her. "What do you think of that offer?"

"I can live with it. But I'd like it better if you were naked beneath me." He thought that was an excellent idea as well. "If I get up and off you for you to undress, you'll let me have my fun, won't you?"

"Absolutely." She got off him, and he watched her as she disrobed. Her body was perfect, he thought. Supple and toned up. He wanted to take her right now. "I do have one request for you, however."

"All right. What is it?" Her eyes darkened and her face flushed with need. "You wouldn't mind if I did the same to you? Swallowed you down the back of my throat."

"No. I said you could have as much fun as you wanted. Remember?" Finally naked, he got back on the bed, his body stretched out before her. When she climbed back up him, using his legs as leverage, he nearly cried out when she held his erection in her hand. "You're killing me."

When she had trouble guiding him into her sheath, he held himself up so that she could slide over him. As soon as he moved past the swollen lips of her pussy, he felt her take him into her like she'd just taken him into her throat. Crying out, she sat over him without moving as he tried to catch his breath.

She rode him as if she'd never done it before. He was happy that she had no more experience, and also thrilled that she hadn't enough practice at it that she killed him. Christ, she was taking his body to heights that he'd never been to before with a woman.

Her hands touched him everywhere she could reach. Sawyer loved it when she sipped at his nipples, tweaked them hard then softly. The sounds that came from her throat were hungry sounding, like she had taken him as a cat.

When Raven began to ride him harder, a little faster, he

watched as she cupped her breasts into her palms. The way she played with her own nipples, making them pinker than before, stiffer too. He wanted to sit up and take the morsels into his mouth, to taste her like she had him, but he'd promised to let her play, and he was going to do it even if it killed him.

Sawyer was on the verge of begging her when she spoke. "Take me, Sawyer. I need to come with you."

The thought did occur to him to make her suffer too, to drag out his taking her until she was begging him as well. But as soon as he flipped her and she wrapped her body around his, her slim legs tightening around his hips, it was all he could do not to pound her hard enough to take his own pleasure, leaving hers until the next time. But he should have known she'd still be the aggressor, even though he was on top of her.

Her body met his with each downward stroke. She moaned each time he pulled her closer to his own body. Taking her mouth, he kissed her with all the need that he had. Raven didn't back off; she gave as good as she got. And when she dug her nails, the claws of her cat, down his back, he cried out. Not in pain, but from the most intense pleasure he'd ever had.

"Come for me." She shook her head, telling him that she needed more. "Come, my love, and I will give you all that I have."

She dug her nails deeper, her body bowing up off of the bed. And when he was ready to sob, to beg her to release, she screamed out his name so loudly that he felt his cat roar back at her. It was then that he bit down on her shoulder and emptied himself deep inside of his mate.

Sawyer took her three more times, bringing her to peak each time he commanded her to come. And when her arms went limp on the bed, he dropped onto her, unsure that he could move for the rest of his life.

When he woke the room was dark except for the moon shining into the window and across the bed. Raven was still asleep, so he just watched her. There were marks on her body, small bruises that he'd put there when he'd gotten too rough. Sawyer knew that she'd heal quickly, so after kissing her creamy shoulder, he got out of the bed.

Not bothering with clothing, he made his way to the basket of fruit. Starving, Sawyer unceremoniously tore the plastic paper off the entire thing. Grabbing two of the apples and a handful of grapes, he turned when the light came on.

"Christ, you are the most beautiful man I've ever seen. If I could paint, I'd paint you as you are now. Naked, with only your fruit to feed you." She grinned at him. "Bring me something too. I'm starving."

Grabbing more of the fruit, he thought about it and shoved all the things he'd taken from it back in and took the entire basket to the bed. Raven pulled the two glasses from the drawer, and he snagged the champagne from the now melted ice as he walked by it.

Climbing onto the bed with her, he thought about getting them a towel so as not to ruin the sheets, but he saw that they'd torn them up a bit when their cats had marked their mates. Grinning, he found a knife buried deep in the basket, and started cutting pieces of apple and feeding them to her.

"I think we're going to owe a deposit or something for this room. We've made a mess of it." She told him that her grandma owned it. "Well, that clears things up. I just noticed that the basket's card said the Addington staff. I guess that's not going to be your staff at your home."

"I'm sure they're planning something. By the way, I was going to ask you something earlier and got sidetracked. My dad has it in his head that he's going to have you come and work for him. While I think that you'd be good at what he has in mind, I was wondering if you could tell him that you'd like to divide your time between his offices and ours." Sawyer told her that he'd not mentioned what he'd be doing. "Oh, sorry. Security. He wants you to get his in shape. There have been a few incidents over the last few months, and it's because the security team was so lacking in knowledge about things. Since he and M other are divorcing, I'm betting that he wants to make sure that she can't get into the place. Not that I think she's ever been there before, but he loves the people that work for him as much as I do."

"I can do that. But I'm not as sharp on it as someone with experience would be. Can I have a couple of those grapes before you eat them all?" Laughing, she fed him some of them like in the pictures he'd seen in the museum once—the man draped out on a couch and a woman feeding grapes to him from above. "I'd like to talk to you about adopting Molly, too. I want her to be my child in name, if you're all right with that."

"I am, but you'll need to speak to her about it as well. That's a big decision, and I think that she should be able to answer for herself." Raven kissed him and laid back on the bed. "I'm stuffed. Exhausted too, I think."

He put the basket on the floor with the now empty bottle, and laid down with her. She was warm, thanks to her cat, and she curled around him as if they were in the deep woods trying to keep warm. Raven asked him to tell her about being a cat.

"I don't know what I could tell you, honey. I've been one all my life, and I wouldn't even know where to begin in telling you about my other half. I can tell you about myself, if you want. Your grandma, she and Molly, gave me a lot of details on you." She told him she doubted any of it was true. "I think everything they told me is true. You're kind and generous. You're also strong, and aren't afraid to step in where there is an extra hand needed. Molly thinks that you're super mom."

"She would. I love that child so much, Sawyer. I never thought, after her father told me that he was married, that I'd love anything or anyone again. It was in my head to put her up for adoption when she was born. But the first time she moved inside of me, I knew that I could never do that to us. Then when Schaller was killed, I started thinking that she'd be my only love. Then you came along." Sawyer pulled her chin up so that he could look her in the eyes. "I didn't think I was going to like you, much less love you, Sawyer. When I found out that you changed me into a cat, I wanted to hate you for that too. But all I could think about was that I'd not died. That I was going to live for a while longer. Falling in love with you was easy after I saw the way you stood up for Molly and myself. My mother is not one to back down when she's cornered."

"Neither am I. I've been around the worst kind of criminals and come out on top. Not always unscathed, but a better man for it. When I retired, it wasn't because I'd had enough of the job, but because I'd had a stupid partner who thought that his way was the only way. He wasn't the first new guy I had, but he ended up being the last. I was not going to be shipped home in a box because some idiot decided that firing his weapon was easier than talking things through." He pulled her closer to his body. "I love you too, Raven. I think I have since the first time I saw you. You were hooked up to machines that were breathing for you, something to keep track of your heart beats, and a couple of machines that I have no earthly idea what they did except sing a song that told me you were alive. Despite all that, I knew from the moment that I saw you in the parking lot of your building that you were my mate."

"Oh, so it's just my money you don't care for, is that it?" He wondered where she'd gotten that. "You told my grandma that we weren't suited to each other because of how we were different classes or some shit. I'll have you know that even though I came from money — we've been rich since way before my mother was born — I've always worked hard. I do a lot of charity works. I donate a great deal of my time and efforts to other —"

He put his hand over her mouth. When she kissed the palm of his hand, he pulled it away and kissed her mouth.

"I love that you have money. Does that calm you down a bit?" She nodded. "I don't know how good I'll be at being rich with you. I mean, I can stand where you tell me. Wear what you want me to. I've become very good at following directions. But I have to have an income. I don't mind helping you and your father out, but I do need to have a job."

"Did you think that you were being asked to do this security detailing because you're married to me?" He told her that he didn't mind doing it, but no, he didn't expect anyone to pay him for it. "Why not? I mean, you're offering us your expertise. Of course you'll be paid."

"It's all right. I don't mind."

He held her to him, hoping that he could change the

subject. He loved that she had money. But for him, it wasn't pride that had him wanting to work. It was the need to feel useful to himself. He didn't think that would go over any better than him doing the work they asked him to do for free. The Addington's were sure funny about their money.

~*~

"Sir, there is a suit there for you to wear should you want. Mrs. Addington said that she'd prefer that you wore it, but you could come as you are." Since Dwayne had no idea what he was going to be doing, he pulled open the box and whistled. "If you don't mind me saying, sir, I think that will look very nice on you. Not many men can pull off a three piece pinstriped suit."

"Thanks." Dwayne was a cat, and not at all shy about his body. Pulling off his clothing, he decided to ask Carl, the driver, what was going to happen today. "I mean, am I going to be a secretary or a mail boy? If you ask me, this suit screams something like a bauble. You know, a younger man to hang on the arm of a very beautiful older woman."

The man nearly wrecked the limo, he was so shocked. Laughing a little as he pulled off his jeans, Dwayne told Carl that he was sorry, but he was very nervous. The pants fit him well, as did the white silk shirt and pants. The shoes were a little tight, so he wore the ones he had on. But he did try and polish them up a bit with his old shirt.

"I believe that you'll be going to meetings with Mrs. Addington at first. She did mention to me that she thought that you'd be a powerhouse in making people see reason." The first thing that popped into his head was that she'd hired him as a hit man, so to speak. Bring out his cat and people would do what she wanted. "She's a good woman, Mrs. Addington.

104

But men tend to see her as a doddering old woman who is only playing at being head of a multi-billion dollar company. Mr. Addington, he knew who ran the company, and would seek her advice on every detail that was brought up. After he died, she sort of lost interest in a great many things, including life. That was until little Miss Molly came along."

"I don't think she needs me as badly as she thinks. I've seen her take command of a room and hold their attention until she made her point." Carl said that she was good at that, but what she lacked, in his opinion, was the nerve to tell a man to sit down and shut up. "So, I'm the heavy in this?"

"I don't know that for sure, but if she sees something in you that made her hire you, then you can bet that you should have been that all your life. Take me, for instance. I was a homeless man just back from a tour of duty. My wife and children had left me. My house was repossessed because as a service man, my checks didn't make it to the bank on time and the bank foreclosed on it. I was ready to chuck it all and be done with it when she picked me up and shook some since into my noodle, and hired me as her driver. She said that a man that had lived on the streets as much as I did must know them pretty well. I did, and we've been working well together since, I think."

"What do you see me as?" He glanced at him in the mirror next to him. Dwayne was trying to get his tie to work, never having worn one before, when he looked at the older man. "That bad, huh?"

"I see you as being anything you wish to be. And if you don't mind me saying so, you could run the company for her and do a good job of it." Dwayne asked if he thought she was going to give him some kind of head job. "I don't know. But as I said, you'll be good at it."

When they pulled to the curb, he was still fussing with his tie. Carl opened the door for him and took Dwayne's tie off him and threw it in the back seat of the limo. Brushing some lint off his coat jacket, he told him he looked fit for any job.

Entering the building, he was met by a woman by the name of Nancy. She looked like one of the schoolteachers that had been in story books he'd read as a child. All she needed to fit the part was a ruler in her hand. She was spouting off things that he was doing today like he knew what the hell he was doing. He put up his hand, and she stopped talking.

"I was to meet Mrs. Addington here this morning." She said that her meeting was where they were headed first. "Okay then. Perhaps you can tell me what it is I'm going to be doing for her."

"She told me to tell you to be yourself. That was what she had hired you for." Dwayne said that he wasn't sure that was going to work, he was a farmer. "Yes, but I'm to understand that you have skills that will suit this company well. Mrs. Holly also said to tell you not to knock, but to come right in as if you own the place. That is what, she told me, you were good at. Taking a passion for something and making it yours."

"I don't understand." They were moving again, and entered an elevator all by themselves even though there were several people waiting. The beautifully decorated cavern shot up the shaft, and they were getting out again in only seconds. Nancy led him to the door. "I don't know what the hell I'm doing here."

"You'll do fine, Mr. Bishop. And if you need anything, just ask anyone for Nancy and I'll be there for you. Your office is on the seventh floor, and your secretary is Lisa James. You do us proud, Mr. Bishop."

She opened the door for him and he was shoved into the room. Christ, he thought, it was a firing squad, and poor Holly was the one blindfolded.

After Dwayne sat down next to her, the meeting resumed. There were several men that eyed him, but none of them asked what the hell he was doing. Dwayne was glad for that, because he wasn't sure how he'd answer them. Opening the notebook in front of him, he read the first line and looked at Holly. She just nodded at the man standing up with a face as red as a fresh apple.

"I don't see what the problem is, Ms. Addington. Your husband would have approved of this move, and you're just holding up the progress of our business. You need to make a firm decision and then—"

"I've told you my decision three times now, Burt, and I'm sticking by it. And my husband would not have agreed to taking all that farmland from the growers and turning it into a shopping mall. He would be rolling over in his grave should I even consider it." The man huffed at her. "There are farmers there that depend on that land for their livelihood. You cannot expect them to be all right with this."

"I still don't see where the problem is. It's land that you own, and there is no reason whatsoever that it should be just lying there with a few tomatoes growing on it for some family to have a bacon, lettuce, and tomato sandwich whenever they want one."

Dwayne wanted to say something, but he wasn't sure he was in any position to say a word. This was a meeting that he'd been literally tossed into, and he didn't want to lose his job on the first day. Holly kept poking him in the leg and he stood up. Not sure how he got to his feet, he just stood there — he'd only meant to move away from her poking finger — but once he was up, everyone stared at him. Burt asked him what the hell he was doing there.

"I work for Holly the same as you. But I have a question for you, sir. You said that you thought that families were only growing tomatoes so that they could have a BLT. Correct?" Burt didn't answer him, but he did roll his eyes. "I'll take that as a yes. Where do you think the food comes from that you had for breakfast this morning? I assure you that it didn't just show up at the grocery store."

"I don't think that, you idiot. Sit down before I sit you down. Christ, now we have teenagers coming in here and talking at meetings. I tell you, Holly, I'm ready to sell my shares and — "

"Sell them, then." Dwayne went to the paper that was hanging on a wall as he continued. "Sell your shares and get out of here. I'm sure this meeting would go a great deal better if you weren't spouting shit you have no idea about. Farmers put the food on your table, every single day of their lives. They don't get time off for holidays, they don't get paid unless someone decides to purchase their crops that they don't put up for themselves. A paycheck doesn't come to them if they sit in meetings and bluster about how things aren't going their way."

Dwayne drew a bushel basket on the paper. Then he drew what he hoped looked like a tractor. Putting the price on the tractor that his father had wanted for years, he put the price of corn under the basket. Then he turned to the room.

"A farmer needs equipment every year to be able to feed you. As you can see by what a bushel of corn costs compared to a tractor, they need a great deal of corn to even be able to purchase the tractor. Then there are other pieces of equipment that will go with it—a seeder, something to plow the ground then cultivate it. Each of these add to the price of the tractor. Some farmers are several hundred thousand dollars in debt before they even put their first seed in the ground." Burt said this wasn't a meeting on the price of corn. "Oh, but it is. You want to take possession of the land that these farmers use. What do you think will happen to them once you do that?"

"They'll have to find other jobs. What do I care? We need to cultivate that land so that we can put in more stores for people to spend money in. I don't know if you realize this or not, but this company pays your salary." Dwayne told him it was the farmers that did that. "And just how do you figure that? You really are a moron, aren't you?"

"You're a nasty prick, but we'll talk about that later. If you take the land from these people, they have no income. Correct?" Burt said that it wasn't any of his business if they had money or not. "You don't think so? Well then, who will be shopping in your stores if they have no money? And if there are no farmers to put the food on their tables, they're going to have to have it imported. It'll cost more, and that will have to be part of the price you pay at the stores. People will no longer have the disposable income they had before. The farmers will have to pay back the hundreds of thousands of dollars on a job that pays nothing much more than minimum wage. After that, they'll need, perhaps, some help from the government. Food stamps will be used more than before. Your taxes, the salary that you had coming in from Holly here, will be used to pay for the stamps, as well as the insurance that they'll need because they can no longer afford to purchase it on their own.

The banks that they borrowed the money from, they'll have to go bankrupt then because — well, they have several million dollars in debt that they can't collect on. Your taxes will go for that as well. You have to understand, Burt, that there is a trickle-down theory in all of this. Just by taking one farm away, you will affect everyone from the janitor at the schools to the teachers that aren't being paid, as there isn't enough income in the towns to pay them. Everything has an effect on everything. You just aren't getting that. And also, you ever call me an idiot or a moron again, I will tear you apart and bury you under a sidewalk so that you're never heard from again."

Dwayne sat down and felt like a fool. When Holly patted him on the leg, he wanted to bolt to the bathroom. He'd just made a fool of himself, and he hated himself for being rude to the other man. There might have been more talk, but Dwayne was too busy beating himself up about what he'd done. He was sure that he'd be unable to show his face around here again.

Chapter 8

Raven was enjoying herself. She'd been to Columbus before, several thousand times, she'd bet, but this was the first time she'd ever looked around. She'd been working so hard that she'd missed seeing the world around her. And being with Sawyer, she saw things through his eyes, like they were both exploring a new city that they had only just discovered.

They bought things for Molly and Grandma. Raven could tell that Sawyer was checking price tags for things, and he usually ended up at the clearance rack before they left the shops. She didn't mind. To be honest, she shopped like that too. Finding the best bargain was what kept her and Molly in clothing year round.

They didn't so much as eat, but grazed things they thought they'd like. There was a street fair going on, one she'd wanted to attend for years but hadn't had the time. Today was a perfect day for it. They collected bags like it was a race. Ate strange foods and drank exotic drinks.

By the time they got back to the hotel they were exhausted.

Taking a nap seemed like a great idea, and she stretched out on the bed with Sawyer. Almost as soon as they were comfortable, she could have sworn that she was sound asleep.

Raven woke up screaming out a climax that startled her. The mouth on her pussy was devouring her, and she wanted so much more of it. Sawyer said that he'd have his turn with her, and he was making short work of making her feel like she was getting more than she had given him.

Sawyer massaged her thighs, her buttocks, as well as her breasts. She needed him inside of her, and no matter how much she begged him to take her, he only continued to eat her. Every time she came, Raven was sure that it was going to be the last that she could have. But as Sawyer continued to take her, the need that she had seemed to be more. She wasn't getting enough from him. When she finally had more than she could suffer, because she felt that she was, she yanked his hair up and looked him in the face.

"Take me now." He shook his head. "You either take me now or I'm going to kill you. I'm sure that it won't go over well with your parents, until I explain to them how you left me hanging."

"You're in heat." It took her befuddled mind several minutes to get what he was saying to her. "As a cat, it's stronger, and if I take you now, you'll carry my child."

"I'm on the pill." He told her that it wouldn't work on her. That as a cat, no meds would work on her unless she took major amounts of them. "You're telling me that if you fuck me right now, I'll carry your child. And it matters little that I'm taking precautions."

"Yes. I was going to talk to you about it, but you looked so delicious laying there all naked and warm. I didn't want to—"

"Take me, Sawyer. Give me your child. Please." Sawyer told her to be sure. There would be no turning back. "I want your child. I want us to raise all of our children, including Molly, to be good responsible people. Please, I want to have your baby."

Sawyer crawled up her, tasting her skin, kissing her in places that she felt were not erotic. Her navel, the underside of her breast. Even her ears and the lobes that were a part of her. When he kissed her, taking his time, making her feel like she was a part of him, Sawyer slid into her and gave her the feeling that she was home, that there was no other place that she wanted to be than with this man.

As they made love, he was gentle with her this time, telling her how much he loved her. How he worshiped everything about her. When he moved finally, Raven cried out, her body coming in a short burst of releases, and she told him how much she loved him.

"And I love you, my dearest wife." He continued to stroke the inside of her, watching her face, seemingly deep in her eyes. When he took her mouth again, this time with more savagery, she came so hard that she had to hold onto him. Then he came.

Raven knew that he was different this time. His body bowed back from hers, his arms taut with strength. His cock didn't pound her this time, but stilled in her so that she felt the moment that his seed connected with her womb.

Nothing in her life could have prepared her for the oneness of their lovemaking. The child that they created was made from love. Raven held him to her, crying for the overwhelming feelings that she was having. Sawyer told her

113

over and over again that she was his, that he belonged to her.

After waking up from their nap, they decided to leave in the morning. They had a lot of things going on, and Raven was looking forward to going back to work. Dinner was their first thought, however, and they decided to celebrate with a large dinner. By the time they found one that they thought would be good, it was nearly nine o'clock.

Her ringing phone had her groaning. Sawyer asked if he could take the call from her mom when she told him who it was. As she got ready, listening to him answer the phone, Raven decided that they'd have a lot of celebrating to do soon, and she couldn't wait to tell Molly she was going to be a big sister.

"Hello, Merriam." While she couldn't hear the other end of the conversation, she could almost guess what her mother was saying. She'd be demanding to speak to her about now. "I'm sorry, but she's currently not taking any calls from you. However, if you'd like to talk to me, I'm all ears." Sawyer put it on speaker phone just as she was ready to take the phone from him when he laughed. "I'm sorry, my dear mother-in-law, could you repeat that please?"

"I said that I'm not speaking to you. That I wish to speak to my only child. You put her on this phone right now. I'll deal with you later." Sawyer told her no. "Did you just tell me no? I'll have you know that I'm not some tart that you screw around with. I'm—"

"Yes, yes, I know, you're an Addington. You'll have to remember that your last name means squat to me. Now, as I have said, Raven is currently busy, but I'll be glad to answer your questions." Mother cursed at him, something that she'd not done in a long while. "My my, I can see now that you have a mouth on you. Not that it matters. It doesn't change the fact that you're not speaking to your daughter. We're having a wonderful honeymoon, and I won't have you messing around with our fun. And just for you, Merriam, I've just made an exception to our little secret. You'll also be happy to know that we're going to make you a grandma again. Perhaps you can refrain from pissing this one off so much that they refuse to speak to you."

"Raven Addington, you had better answer me. I know darn good and well that you're listening in on this call with the moron you think you married. I need to talk to you. You are not going to have this man's baby. What are you thinking? And your father has filed for divorce, and I want you to talk him out of it. You and he have always conspired together, so you should be good at doing this for me. It's the least you can do after all I have suffered from you and your stupidity." Raven looked at Sawyer and smiled at him. "Raven? I swear to you if you don't answer me, I'm going to—"

"I can hear you, Mother. If you think you're going to get any brownie points with me by calling my husband a moron, then you're sadly mistaken. You're also mistaken when you say I'm not going to have this baby. Believe me, I will. And I'm not talking Dad out of anything. In my opinion, he should have done this long ago." Mother cursed again. "What do you want? I'm having a good time, and I don't want to have you spoiling it for me. Speak up, then leave me alone."

"Is this because I smacked that illegitimate child of yours? Raven, you have to understand what sort of pressure I've been under of late. You would know if you were to pay any attention to me. But I guess that's the way it goes. You made your mistakes, Raven, not I, and taking this man as your husband, you have to know that it's not going to last. You're going to be bored with him almost before the ink dries on your license. Break it off now and speak to your father for me, and I'll try and get along with that child."

"Her name is Molly, and there will soon be two children." Mother huffed, then said Molly was a common name. "I guess you would know all about common names, wouldn't you, Mother? Dad told me that you were nothing but a waitress at a gambling establishment when he found you."

"That is not true, and I'd appreciate it if you didn't spread such lies about me. I've had a hard enough time keep up appearances for what you've done to the family name without you going around and spreading more of your silly gossip." Mother took a deep breath and let it out slowly. "Now, about this meeting that you're going to have with your father. I'd like to be there, but I can understand why I shouldn't be. I don't want anyone to make a scene, and I'm sure that your father will. He has no regard for how much we must make our names flawless. You talk to him and tell him that I'm the backbone of our marriage, and that he needs me to be there for him. I can just imagine the house now. He's more than likely fired all the people that I hired, and has redone all the rooms to suit himself."

"You've only been gone from his life...well, I was going to say only a few days, but you've been out of his thoughts for a lot longer than that, haven't you?" Mother huffed at her again. "I'm not going to do anything you've said. You're wasting my time and your own if you think I'm going to do anything for you." She asked her why not. "Well, for beginners, you slapped my daughter and then me. I don't think that is very endearing, do you?"

116

"You needed it. And so did that child of yours. I swear, Raven, you have no idea what it's like to be me." Raven told her that she was glad for that. "What a thing to say to me. Why, I'm the only reason that you're still a member of good standing at the club where I go. Not to mention, I've been looking for you a good husband, one that doesn't wear cowboy boots to the dinner table. You should be thanking me rather than putting me down."

"I've never asked you to do those things. And just a reminder, I'm already married, and plan to still be married long after you're dead and gone. As far as being a member of your club, Mother, I canceled my membership a long time ago. You, I've noticed, fit right in with the women there. All of them are snippy fools that only think of one thing, and that's how much money their husbands make for them to spend." Mother said they were her best friends. "And that is exactly my point. You're all alike. From your 'Let me talk to the manager' haircut to the way you order people around when you think you've been slighted somehow. Well, I'm over it. And so you know, now that I'm married, I plan on staying away from the place forever. I won't have dinner with you there. No more luncheons, nor will I be attending any more of your little bitch sessions there. I've better things to do with my time than to snip at Patty Joe Bangles, or whoever isn't at the table, on how she wears her hair now that you're all sheep and have the same hairdo."

Looking at Sawyer, who looked like he was ready to bust something to keep from laughing, she cut her hand across her throat for him to hang up. Her mother was still talking, but she no longer cared. She wanted her to leave her alone now that she had someone in her life that treated her with respect and loved her.

"My dear, can you tell me what a 'I want to talk to the manager' haircut is?" He laughed harder. "All I can see is a bunch of women standing in line at the returns counter looking like clones of each other and saying the same thing — 'I want to talk to your manager' — in a monotone voice that sounds the same with all of them." She told him it was just like that with her mother's friends. "I guess I need to pay better attention to haircuts now. I'm assuming that you don't belong to the club for that reason."

"No, I don't belong there because I was paying to be a member yet I never went there. It was just easier to go to lunch or whatever in town rather than to drive there and have my membership inspected every time. Not to mention, they have a dress code that I never seemed to meet." Sawyer asked her if she ever tried. "No. Why should I? I was paying them to allow me to eat there, then pay dues every year and not get a thing from it. Just so I could say that I belonged? No thanks. Are you ready to go eat?"

He was still laughing when they entered the elevator. She wasn't sure if she wanted to join him in his humor or to ignore it. Finally she just gave in and joined him. Raven wasn't going to let her mom mess up her nice honeymoon with the *moron*.

~*~

Roger was glad to hear from Raven. She told him how she'd heard from her mother and that they were coming back tomorrow. He was working on taking care of the first trouble, and glad that he could see the young couple sooner than anticipated.

He'd never realized before how much he missed just talking to her. Usually her mother would be in the background of their conversations telling him to say this or that to her. Meeting her for dinner or something was usually met with the same disregard for him having a nice talk with his daughter. He'd been having fun with Molly too, now that she wasn't afraid to come to his home anymore. And he'd gotten her to call him Grandpa instead of Mr. Addington.

Roger had always wondered why Merriam used their name, a proper noun, like it was a weapon or a shield to others. She would say their last name like she'd been the only one that had ever said it correctly or even used it the way that she did. Merriam assumed that it opened doors for her, when all along it was his mother's name that did everything for the rest of them.

It wasn't as if he didn't do his share of work too. He'd been working since he'd been a young man, following his father all over the building that he'd worked in until he thought his feet would drop off. But it had taught him a great deal. Like the power of money, and also, the downfall that it could cause someone.

"Grandpa Roger, I was wondering something." He asked Molly, who was sitting at his desk with him, what she'd been thinking about. "I have these friends that live near Sawyer that are losing their mom. I've only seen her one time, but she looks pretty bad."

"That's nice, honey." He read the stock report on how his stocks were doing as he half listened to Molly. When she didn't say anything more, he turned and looked at her. It was like having Raven look at him when he wasn't entirely focused on what she'd been saying. "I'm sorry, honey. What's wrong with your friends' mom?"

"She has cancer. Mr. Little, that's their name, has a hard

time keeping his job because he has two kids that he cares for and his wife. Grandma Sippy said that it's a sad thing to happen just because they didn't have the money for insurance, and missed her being sick for too long." He asked her what she wanted to do. "I'm not really sure. I want to make it easier for them. Like have someone come to their home and help Mr. Little out. Did I tell you that he's a computer engineer? He told me once that he can make a computer sing. But not so much lately since he's been out of work. He wasn't begging me for anything. He's like you, Grandpa Roger, he just tells it like it is." Roger asked Molly if she thought that would help them out. "Yes. He can find him a job so that he can have insurance in case one of the kids get hurt. Todd told me that it's too late for his momma. I think they're waiting on her to pass on now. It's so sad."

"It really is." Roger asked for the man's name and decided to have him looked up. He didn't want anyone scamming his granddaughter. But if he could help someone out, he'd do that too.

Picking up his phone, he called his attorney to ask him to look into his job skills as well. Before he could measure up the next column of stocks, he was getting a call back. Roger looked at Molly when he heard that the missus had passed away not an hour ago.

"I've sent flowers, sir, with yours and Molly's name on them. As well as I've had a meat tray and some other items sent to the home. The couple barely had anything to call their own, and the funeral has been paid for by your mother. She also made sure that they had money for any other extras that they might need." He asked him about Mr. Little's job skills. "He's the best there is, sir. I mean, if he's looking for a job,

I'd surely hire him for you. He not only has computer skills, but his ability to put fire walls up and keep them there is legendary."

"How is it that he's not working from his home for someone? I mean, with a sick wife and two children, someone would have snatched him up." Berry explained. "So his home is a rental and he cannot afford to get Internet. Whoever fired him should be reminded that it's the little guy that keeps us going. Hire him. Not today, but soon. Find him a good solid home with enough bedrooms in it for him to have live in help. Also, set him up with a computer –"

Molly shook his arm. Roger asked her what she needed. "He told me that he can build him a computer at a better price, as well as it would work better than anything that he could buy. He just needs the parts, he told me." Molly smiled at him and kissed him on the cheek. "You're a good man, Grandpa Roger."

She left him and he told Berry what he needed. "I can do that, sir. I guess he's thinking of moving back to his wife's family for help with his finances, as well as the children. I'll get on this as soon as I think it's a good time. You are a good man, sir." Embarrassed, he thanked the other man. "I have two homes in mind, sir, that I think will work out for him. Also, I would suggest a car as well as some cash, so that he might be able to get himself the items that he needs to set himself up."

"Yes, the car sounds wonderful for him. Also, I'd like to have the house furnished for them. Not too extravagant, but something plain that they can work with when things settle down. A cook, they'll need a cook too." Berry was making notes and said he'd take care of it. "Something else I'd like for you to do for me, Berry, is to make sure that all the phone numbers are changed for my family's personal numbers."

"Yes, sir. Mr. Bishop's phone has arrived, and I've had it set up with numbers that he'll need. I'll just have to change the one for your daughter when I get hers." After hanging up, Berry called him right back. "Sir, I've just heard from the country club. They wish to know if your wife still has access, as you have cancelled your membership."

"Yes. Wait, no. I want you to set up a membership for myself. And also one for Sawyer and Raven. They will be able to rub it in Merriam's face that they go there and she can't. Also, find out if you can get lessons for Sawyer on how to play golf. I think I'd enjoy a round or two with him just to have a nice long talk." Berry said that according to Sawyer's background check, he did know how to play. He'd taken classes at college. "Good. Hopefully he's not better at it than I am."

They were both laughing when they hung up again. Roger decided that there had to be something he could do with Molly rather than sit in his office all evening. Putting things back where he'd gotten them from, Roger went in search for his granddaughter. He also needed to tell her about Mrs. Little.

Roger found Molly in the kitchen with Ms. Bea. She was making bread for dinner and talking to Molly about clothing. He wasn't sure what they were meaning until Ms. Bea said that Molly could just keep some things at this house so that she'd not have to bring a suitcase every time she came by.

"I don't know if that will work for my mom. She'll say it's a waste to have a set of something here when I'm not here very often. Even if I came here every week, she'd tell me that

I should bring what I have. Mom is very practical." Ms. Bea laughed, and Roger covered his own laughter up when Molly spoke. "I think I'd like to have some things here, however. Like a bathing suit and a towel. I don't think she'll care too much about that, do you?"

"Your momma is a good women, Miss Molly. And that great grand-mammy of yours, she's a hoot to have round too. You are a lucky little girl to have such powerful outspoken women in your family." Molly asked Ms. Bea if Ms. Addington was outspoken. "Well, I'd say she is, but nobody you'd want to be like. I don't like to talk about someone in a bad way, but you'd be better off steering clear of your Grandma Merriam, child. She'll roast you for dinner."

He started to enter, but paused when Molly spoke again. Her voice was very low, but he could hear her well enough. "She doesn't like me. Once, just before Mom was hurt, she took me to that club that she's always going on about. Ms. Addington told them that I was a bastard child of my loose mom. I had to ask Todd what that meant. It's not very nice, is it?" Ms. Bea said for her to ignore it. "I will. But she was really mean to me after that. I guess because the ladies she was talking to thought that Ms. Addington shouldn't say stuff like that in front of me. Ms. Addington said that I was as dumb as a post, and just like my grandpa Roger. Then she hit me when we were going out to the car. It really hurt. I'm so glad that Daddy Sawyer didn't see the big bruise she gave me. He would have been very mad at her."

Roger felt his heart crumble at hearing that. The other day when Merriam had hit Molly, it hadn't been the first time. And he'd bet anything that if she was still around her, it wouldn't have been the last time that Merriam hit her either.

123

Clearing his throat, he entered the kitchen and pretended like he hadn't been eavesdropping. "Ms. Bea, just how far are you into making dinner for us?" She winked at him, and he knew that she'd been aware that he'd heard every word. "I'd like to take Molly for some pizza. I've not had any in a good long time, and I think it would be a real treat for the two of us."

"What a wonderful idea, sir. Why, if that's what you're going to do, I think my man and I will have a cookout. Might not have too many days left for those. You two go on ahead and have yourself a fine night out, and me and the mister will have us some wieners and brats. I surely do love a good hot tater salad too."

When they were out waiting on the car, Molly asked him if he ever drove anymore. Thinking that she had a good idea, he told the driver that he and Molly were on a date, and that he'd escort Molly around in his own car. As soon as he was beneath the wheel, he felt like he could enjoy this again. The reasons for not driving himself were vague to him now as he drove into town for a slice of hot pizza with all the toppings.

He might just make a habit of this, he thought with a grin. Having himself a pizza with his favorite little girl, and perhaps seeing a good movie. Or a bad one. He didn't care so long as he was getting his life in order and spending the day with Molly. Roger thought that he'd been a fool for far too long, and would enjoy the rest of his life from now on.

Chapter 9

Sawyer was having a difficult time wrapping his mind around the size of their house. Christ, he could easily fit three or four of his parents' house in the first floor and still have room left over. He stood in what he assumed was the library and looked at the shelves of books.

"Sir, I can answer any questions you might have about the household. The young miss has returned as well, and is wanting to give you a tour after she has her dinner." He asked why she wasn't eating with them. "I'm not sure. I mean, she usually eats in the kitchen nightly, as her mother works late."

"I don't know how much say I have in changing things up, but if her mother or myself is home, I'd like to have dinner with her. If it doesn't cause a problem." The man hid his grin well, but Sawyer caught it. "So, if she can hold off to have dinner with Raven and I, you can send her in here. By the way, does she need breadcrumbs to get around like I think I will?"

"You'll do fine, sir. Mrs. Bishop is on the phone with her

father. If you would like to wait on her as well, I'm sure that the three of you will have a very good time." Thanking him, not remembering his name, Sawyer wondered if it would be rude for him to ask that they wear name tags on their uniforms as well as what part of the house they cared for. So far, he'd met four different people that cared for different parts of the household — including, he only just remembered, the outbuildings. Sawyer very much doubted that they had the same type of outbuildings as he had on the farm.

"Hello, Dad." He grinned at Molly when she entered the room with him. "I've been practicing saying that. I love the way it sounds, don't you?"

"I think it's been my favorite sentence said to me. How was your weekend with your Grandda Roger?" Sawyer felt stupid calling a grown man, nearly twenty years older than him, Grandda Roger. "I heard that you had a great time on your date with him."

"We did. I think you might say that we're getting to know each other. Ms. Addington never let me hang out with them when we visited. She said that children were never to be seen or heard in a household. Which I thought was really mean. What are you looking for in here?" He told her a way out. "You're funny. I can show you around. Mom said that she'd be a little while longer on the phone. She missed a lot of stuff, I guess."

"I bet she did. What rooms are off limits?" Molly looked confused. "This is a big house. I'm assuming that Raven has some rooms that are specifically her own. You understand. Rooms that no one is allowed to enter."

"No, Mom lets me in any room I want so long as I clean up after myself. I bet you have to do that too. Want to see the upstairs?" As soon as Molly put her hand into his, he felt that he could have followed her anywhere. "Mom and I have the two bedrooms at the end of the hall. That way I can come in and snuggle with her when I want. Are you a snuggler, Dad?"

"I've been known to snuggle up as often as I can. Your mom, she told you that we were cats. Cats are very close animals." She asked if she could see his cat sometime. "I would imagine that you'll be seeing him a great deal."

She took him into her room first. He had expected it to be pink, he had no idea why, but the room wasn't quite as bad as he had thought it would be—just a spot of the color here and there. But it was the bed that captured his attention. The big oak four poster bed had a lacy canopy as well as a white lacy cover. He looked around and decided that this house was perfect for Molly and Raven.

"I used to have a computer, but I got into trouble with it. I shouldn't have been messaging people personal stuff. It wasn't as bad as it sounds, but Mom freaked out about it, saying that I was just too young to be talking with boys that might be men." Sawyer said that he'd run into some people that pretended to be boys, when they were actually monsters. "That's what Mom said. There are all kinds of monsters, and not all of them look or sound like they really are."

"Your mom is absolutely right about that." Raven entered the room just as he said that. While Molly told her mom why she was right, he looked around the room for security issues. He could see so many in this room that it frightened him a little. "If you don't mind, I'd like to make some changes to the house. Just in the event that someone comes around and they're not welcome."

"Please do." He told her of the few things that he'd seen in this room alone. "I can see that you're going to be perfect for what Dad has in mind for you. I would never have thought of the window in the bathroom being an issue. I mean, it is on the third floor. But you're right. If someone can see out, then someone can see in too. I want to feel safe in our home."

They walked around the entire upstairs, looking in each of the spacious five bedrooms, not counting the master bedroom. Curtis, their butler, gave him a notebook and a pen after finding them in the main hall again. Raven had asked him to bring things when he had time. The man was very loyal, Sawyer could see.

He began making notes on things like windows and locks on the doors. When Raven showed him the safe room, he was both impressed and afraid of the way it had been left open. Sawyer explained why it needed to be closed up and kept secret, and made notes about it as well.

"The door leading in here is made so that no one from the outside can see that the room is here. By leaving the door open, anyone can see the room and what it might be used for. While having a cot and water in here is great, there should also be a medical kit as well as any medications that you might be taking. Small food items too would be nice. You never know how long you might be stuck in a place like this." He smiled at his women as they took what he was saying seriously. "You have a great many things in there that most would not think about. A bathroom is wonderful. Clothing is nice so that you don't have to stink. And its own power grid and telephone is an amazing addition too. Cell phones tend not to work in steel rooms. This room would be a good place to come if you can't get out of the house if there is a fire too."

The master bedroom would have to wait. Dinner was

ready, they'd been told, and they made their way down the stairs again. Raven had her office on this floor, and she thought he'd need one too. He wasn't sure what he'd put in his office, but thanked her for thinking of him. It was a good idea, he told her, to have their offices off the main floor. No one would be accidently walking into the rooms if there were things on the desk that were private.

Gunner was in the dining room when they entered. Hugging his brother, Sawyer asked him to stay for dinner. Curtis assured them there was plenty. After agreeing, he asked him if everything was all right. Gunner nodded and sat Molly on his lap when she asked.

"Yes. I have two weeks to go, then I'm finished. Nothing is wrong, just wanted to see if you could maybe put in a good word here or there for me to find myself a job." Raven asked him what it was he was good at. "Killing people."

"It's not that I don't believe you, but perhaps you could find another way to state what it is you're in the job hunting arena for." Raven smiled at Gunner as she continued. "How are you about security? My dad has taken Sawyer to have a look around his offices. Perhaps, if you want to work for me, you could do the same for me."

"I'm not all that good with people. And I tend to think of everyone as an adversary. If you can live with that, then I can work for you. I just need you to be aware that I carry a gun all the time. Even if you take my gun from me, I'm still going to be armed with things just as deadly." Raven told Gunner he was a cheery man to talk to. "You have no idea. By the way, congratulations on your getting married. If you don't mind, I'd like to have a sample of each of you so that in the event you're...lost, I can find you faster."

Raven shivered and said that if it was okay with Sawyer, she was all right with it. Gunner nodded just as the salads were brought to the table. Instead of eating it, Gunner shoved it away and talked about what he was looking for in a place to live too.

"The job comes with housing if you want it. It's not in the building—we didn't think that was a smart way to go. But it's a nice big house with plenty of yard space. There is staff too, and that is necessary in case you're called away for something. I'm guessing you don't have a great deal of furniture." Gunner said he only had his knapsack. "I'll take that as a no. I don't know if the house is furnished or not, but I'll make sure that you have what you need. The rest we can deal with as we go along."

"You're just going to hire me. No background check or anything." Raven told him that Grandma had all of them checked out when she'd asked Sawyer to watch over her. "I see. And you found a great deal, did you? About me, I mean. Most of it is true, just to let you know."

"I don't doubt that it is, Gunner, but I never read the reports. And had I known your parents like I do now, there would have been no reason for the checks." He told her that was a stupid reason not to check. "Perhaps, but I have my reasons too. I've met them, you see, and there isn't a finer family around. You were raised by good people."

"I'm sure that could be said about a great many mass killers." As Curtis was directing the new staff on how to lay the plates in front of them, Gunner stood up, moved Molly, and had a knife at the throat of Curtis. When neither of them moved, Gunner laughed. "You have a death wish for your butler, or do you trust that easily? And stupidly, I might add."

"No, neither of those. But if you'll look around right now there is a gun at the back of your head, and there are two more that are aimed at you from the doorways." Sawyer nodded when Gunner looked at him. "I'm not stupid, nor do I do things so blindly. Sawyer and I have a great deal of money that I'm sure others would just love to take from us. Everyone that works for me can not only handle a gun, but they are armed at all times. No one will leave this house with one of my family, nor my staff, if I can help it. Now please, have a seat and tell me about yourself, Gunner. I think Molly would also like to call you Uncle. Is Gunner your first name?"

"It is." He sat down and looked around the room then. Not only was there a gun at the back of his head, it was the cook who was holding it there. The two men with guns were dismissed when Gunner sat down. "I'm impressed, Raven. And when you get to know me more, you'll learn that I do not impress easily. Welcome to the family."

They talked throughout the meal, nothing earth shattering, but just lighter things like the weather, the office that Gunner would be working from. Dwayne was mentioned a couple of times, and how Holly was proud of his first day. Sawyer decided that he'd see about that as well. Things were going nicely. Sawyer was sure there was going to be something or someone that came along that would fuck it all up for them.

"Would you like to spend the night here, Gunner?" Sawyer knew his brother would turn Raven down. "All right. But I want you to feel you can come here whenever you want. There will always be a room ready for you, and a bed you can sleep in."

"I'm not good with people, as I said." Raven nodded and told him she wasn't people; she was his sister. "I'm not an easy

131

man to be around either. I've been out in the fields of different countries since I turned nineteen. One year of that can change a man. I've been doing it for a lot longer than that."

"I'm sure that you were good at it too. But you're family to us, and I want to make sure that you have someplace to go when it gets to be too much." He nodded and looked around. "There is a house at the end of this property. It has heat and air, all the amenities that anyone could need. A lake to catch your dinner in, as well as an orchard that is being picked right now. I want you to consider it yours."

"I don't want a home, Raven. I'll be fine." She just stared at him, and Gunner looked away first. "I might take you up on it. Not now, but sometime."

After handing him the keys to the house and the boat house, Raven hugged Gunner and then left the two of them alone. Gunner watched Molly and Raven head to the upper floors, then looked at him.

"She cares about me." Sawyer said that he did too. "You have to or I'll kick your ass, but she doesn't have to and she still cares. I think I might take her up on the job as well as the house. Will that be all right with you?"

"Having you around any way that I can is always all right with me."

They hugged again and Gunner went out the door and disappeared into the darkness. Sawyer thought they'd be seeing a good deal more of him soon, and he was looking forward to it.

~*~

Wesley pulled the tractor into the barn. Getting off, careful of the steam it was blowing off, he felt his heart break for the old man. He'd thought of this particular machine as a person since he'd been old enough to reach the pedal on it.

"I hate to bring this up, Old Man, but I had a few more rows to plow up. Couldn't you have had your hissing fit tomorrow or the next day?" Putting his hand on the hood of the hot engine compartment, he laid his forehead there as well. "I don't know what we're going to do now, buddy. It's not your fault. You're a great deal older than I am. Hell, I think you're older than my dad or his dad."

"Do you normally talk to machinery?" He looked up when a man he didn't know spoke. "You don't know me, but I'm a friend of Holly and Raven Addington. Well, Holly Addington. You must be Wesley Bishop. My name is Cartwright, William Cartwright."

He didn't move from his position at the tractor, but waited there to see what the man would do. Wesley was just tired enough that he'd kill the man so he'd not have to mess with him if he caused him any trouble.

"Can you do that thing? You know, where you reach out to someone and ask them about me? I know that you're a tiger—hell, I can see him racing all over your body. If you'd not have me for dinner and call out to...fuck. What's his name? Your brother. You're freaking me out— Sawyer. Can you contact Sawyer?"

Wesley didn't move but did reach for his brother.

Yes, I sent him. He was supposed to arrive tomorrow. I'm sorry I didn't tell you sooner, Wes. I'm school shopping. What the fuck does a little girl need a calculus calculator for? She's eleven, for fuck— Wesley said his brother's name. *Yes, sorry. His name is William Cartwright. He's got some equipment for you. It's from Holly. She's working on a project, and she needs you to do what you normally do when you get the fields ready for next year.*

Old Man just died on me. I won't be able to fix — Did you say *he had some equipment for me?* Sawyer laughed and said that he had. *And this guy, the one that is about to piss his pants, he brought me what, Sawyer? A shovel to bury my tractor with? I don't have time for this. I have to see if I can kludge together something to get him running again.*

Talk to him. Or, I have a better idea. You come here and shop with my wife and daughter, and I'll talk to him. I swear to you, this is a lot of fun. Wesley smiled and told him he was on his own. *I wonder if Mom will come help me.*

He closed the connection to his brother and moved toward William. The man hadn't lowered his hands, but he did back up. Wesley thought it looked like he was more than just a little afraid of him.

"I talked to Sawyer." William let out a long breath. "He said that you had something for me. I have to tell you, buddy, your timing couldn't be any worse. I don't have time to look through catalogs. I don't want to hear a sales pitch about this new tractor or what you think I can use it for. I need to — Holy fuck, that's a tractor."

William was talking quickly now that he figured he wasn't going to be eaten. Wesley climbed up on the end of the trailer and onto the gleaming tractor that was there. It didn't have tires, but actual treads that moved along three gears. The seat wasn't hard on his ass from years and years of wear and tear.

It had an air conditioner setting. Wesley thought that would be nice, having a nice cool breeze over his face during the hottest part of the season. There was even a small fridge for drinks, he discovered as he poked around on it.

"This is the newest model. I don't even think it was shown in the last farmer's fair." Wesley asked him if there really was a farmer's fair. "Yes, sir. Every year. You have an invitation to attend from now on. As well as tickets to get in, accommodations, and air fare." Wesley knew that it was just a scam, for him to buy this thing. Like he had the money for it. "Mrs. Addington, she said that she'd call you this evening after you took it for a spin. Also, she said for me to take a picture of you sitting on it as proof of you receiving it. She said you'd never sign for it."

"Damn right I won't. Who are you delivering this to?" He'd only been half listening to the man. Mostly he wasn't listening to him at all. Wesley looked at William when he spoke. "I'm sorry. I missed something. A lot of somethings if you just said that this was paid for and mine. I'm not rich. My brother is, but not me."

"Be that as it may, Mr. Bishop, the tractor is yours, along with all the other pieces that will be delivered in the morning. I'm a day early, or it would have arrived with the other implements." Wesley got down off the tractor and took the paperwork for the tractor. "It's all paid for, as you can see. As well as maintenance for the next fifty years. Longer if you need it. My boss was so thrilled to have Mrs. Addington call that he said he'd service it forever."

"You're serious." William nodded and asked for the picture. "Sure. I guess I can do that. You're really leaving this here? And the rest of it is coming tomorrow?"

"The rest of the pieces are coming tomorrow, yes. I don't know what all of them are, sir, but I know one of them is a post hole digger. I got to use the new one we got in with yours. Man, does it do the job."

Wesley got up on the tractor again. What the hell was he going to have to do for this stuff?

135

After the man left, pulling his now empty trailer, Wesley pulled a chair off the porch and sat down in it to stare at his new tractor. He thought about calling Holly and talking to her, but he was terrified, to be honest. What if she told him it had been a joke? A cruel one, but a joke all the same.

At lunch he went into the house, made him a sandwich, and sat back down in his chair. He forgot his drink, and was happy that his mom brought him out a glass of lemonade. She asked him what he was doing.

"I'm not sure, to be honest, Mom. I received this while you were at the grocery. And I'm not sure that I want to find out if it's really mine or not." He handed her the paperwork when she asked for it. "I know that it has my name on it, but do you have any idea how much this thing costs? Brand new? Not to mention, according to this, there are seven other pieces coming with it."

"And with this paperwork saying that it's paid in full, that you're not responsible for fixing it and that you needed it, you still don't believe it?" Wesley nodded, and she popped him in the back of the head. "Get up off your fanny and get back to work. Whoever you think might have gifted you with this and then they're going to take it away, don't you think you should get as much work out of it as you can before they do?"

Wesley looked at his mom and smiled. "Have I told you lately how wonderfully brilliant you are? You are the smartest woman—no, the smartest person that I have ever known. And I know a great many of them." Another pop to his head. "I love you, Mom."

He got up on the tractor and laughed. There was a phone on it, with GPS. Yelling to his mom, not as loudly as he'd have had to with Old Man, he told her that she could call him. Waving him off, she went into the kitchen to do her magical things in there.

As he drove out to the field where Old Man had left him hanging, Wesley played around with the plows that came on this sucker until he got the hang of it. He nearly fell off the back of the thing when he engaged the plow and pushed the gas pedal to the floor, as he'd had to do for Old Man. Christ, it was fast.

The jingling of something had Wesley thinking that he'd broken it already. But he saw the phone again, and it was flashing a green light. Picking up the phone, he realized that his mom had remembered the number, as it was her voice that was laughing about something when he answered.

"It's yours. I just had a long talk with Holly. She and your brother are working on keeping farmland free of people putting in malls. I guess Dwayne did a bang-up job in talking this guy into giving up his shares to pay Holly back, and she wants to use you as a poster boy or something." He asked her what that meant as he turned his tractor around to do some of the places he'd not been able to plow because of the other tractor just not having it in him. "She said that she wants to be able to show people how, if farmers have the right equipment and funds to keep them updated, the world will be a better place. I could have told her that myself and she'd not have needed to send you that thing. Are you being safe?"

He wasn't, but he wasn't telling his mom that. Wesley was having fun despite having to replough all the work he'd done today. And he was doing it in about half the time. After telling her that he was, they hung up.

Wesley looked over what he'd done compared to what

he done earlier today. The dirt was churned up nicely. No huge parcels that looked like they had only been half done. The grass that he fought year round was also gone on the new ploughing. Turning off the big rig, he walked the land and noticed that it looked richer, like it was ready for new planting. Wesley had an idea as he drove back to the barn.

He could plant winter wheat this year. He'd never had the means to do that before. The tractor was barely making it after a single season. But with this, he could not just put in wheat, but he could also get the ground around the house better worked up. Mom had wanted a pea garden for years, but he'd not been able to make Old Man break through the packed dirt enough to make it work.

Going into the house, Wesley saw his dad sitting at the table looking at seed catalogs. They received them every fall, but this was the first time his dad had ever looked at them as far as he knew. Grabbing himself and his dad a glass of water, they studied the seeds as well as talked about what they could plant in the coming months.

"I'm going to be able to put in Mom's pea garden. I'm going to do it tomorrow for her." Dad smiled at him and handed him a note. Mom had gone into town to help out with the Little children for the mister. Wesley laughed at what his mom had written down. "She says that she'd like to be able to put out ten rows of peas, as well as have a place for her flowers around the house. I think we can handle that, no problem."

"Son, do you have any idea how this is going to help us and the other farmers around here? I mean, you'd have time to plow our ground up and do theirs too without things for us being put back too far." He told his dad about the ground he'd worked up. "My goodness. That's a wonderful thing, isn't it? Maybe, if you've some room up in that thing, I'll take a ride with you. It would be nice to be able to sit on something that nice."

As Wesley was heading up to bed, he thought of something else he wanted to put in. His mom had always envied the roses around the courthouse. She'd drive there every summer just to look at them and to take a few pictures. He was going to plough her up some place for her to start her own.

Knowing next to nothing about roses, he decided to ask Holly about them. A woman like her would have a gardener, of course, but surely she knew something about the pretty blooms. Making himself a note, Wesley was going to talk to her, right after he gave his dad a ride in the new rig. Yes, it was very nice having nice things.

But he wasn't going to take advantage of Holly's good nature. He'd do just about anything for the wonderful woman. Wesley would do this project for her, happily. Even if she'd not given him the right tools to make it work, he would have anyway. But this way made it a great deal easier.

Chapter 10

Raven moved from one office on her floor to the next, getting information and asking questions. There were things going on that could wait until later to be done, but that wasn't in her nature. She wanted things done early so that if there was trouble, she had plenty of time to fix it.

Sara Becker, her secretary, was on the phone when she passed her desk. Bypassing her, she made her way into her office and one of the three computers that she had set up.

"Why don't you just add all the programs to one computer, and that way you won't have to jump around your office like a jack in the box?" She smiled at her grandma. "I swear, hanging around your dad and Sawyer is like running a race where I know I cannot win. How are you, darling? Are you getting back into things?"

"I am. And the reason that I have three separate computers is because it makes me feel more organized. This one is for inventory. The one on my desk is for emails and correspondence. The third one is for emails coming in from clients that want to speak to me about something I can do for them." Sara brought in phone call message slips and two glasses of tea, one for her and Grandma. "Are they getting along all right, Dad and Sawyer? When he left the house this morning, I was sure he was never going to return. Molly and I had this huge fight, and he was caught in the middle of it."

"Good heavens. What on earth were you fighting about? I was sure that child never got upset about anything. What did you do to her?" Raven just looked at her grandma. "I know, dear. It's not always your fault. But you have to agree that she's very well adjusted."

"She is. But there is a swim party going on at her school, and she doesn't want to go. She wants to hang out with Todd and Jane. I told her that I had to meet their parents first and she threw a fit. Something about me not paying attention to her when she talked. I know I would have remembered her mentioning their names. And by the time we got around to their names, Sawyer was gone. Do you know these children?"

"Yes. You know of them too. They just lost their mother. Mrs. Little." Raven felt her heart break more for them. "She wants to spend time with them, I'm betting, so they can be normal again. From what I've heard, their home is being packed up. The things that they grew up with are being left behind."

"I didn't know their last name. I don't think we got that far before she took off to her room." Grandma said that she was taking it pretty hard too. "I would imagine. I'll talk to her when I get home. Why are their things being left behind?"

"I had no idea that the house was a rental, and that it had been furnished too. As soon as they're out of the house, I'm going to have an inspector go over there and see what sort of things those people have been living with. The landlord, whoever he is, should be made to live in that shack. It's a mess. Thomas said that he'd been calling him all the time for the roof. It's literally falling down on their head. The shower doesn't work, and the tub drains out the water as fast as it's filled up. Poor little mites. To have to have their momma suffering like she was, and to live like that. I'm so glad that Roger is putting them someplace safer and nicer."

"Dad told me that Thomas is a computer expert. That he can build a computer to my specs much cheaper than it would be for us to buy one that would only do half of what his would." Grandma said that she'd heard that too. "Neither Sawyer nor I got to go to the funeral. There wasn't any mention of it in the paper. Plus, there was only a graveside service for her. Dad said he wished that he could have gone as well. You went, I heard."

"Yes. Pitiful show of one's life, if you ask me. That woman lived in this area for her entire life, and only three people besides me and the director were there. I never thought of it not being in the paper. But at the house there was plenty of food and flowers. I don't know how they do things around here when someone passes, but I can tell you that those women sure did want Thomas to know they were single and loved his children." Raven thought that was gross. "So did I. But you have to remember that these are farm people. They need a man, or so they've been raised to think, that'll give them sons to take care of them in their golden years. Also to plant and bring in the food that they eat. Just what I've been working on with Dwayne. He's a pepper pot, I'll tell you that."

"Grandma, you're sounding more and more like Saul every day. Speaking of which, that man and Wesley have been looking over seed catalogs. I have no idea why I thought that they just used last year's seeds, but I guess there are things they have to buy every year. But they're going to put a few rose beds in for Sippy. And peas. Did you know that peas should be planted on Saint Paddy's day? Or was that potatoes? I don't know, but they have to be in the ground early because they don't care for hot weather." Grandma laughed at her. "Yes, well, when you live with a family of farmers, you get to know all kinds of tidbits like that."

Grandma stood up and picked up her pocketbook. Another term that she'd learned from Sippy — pocketbook, not purse.

"I'm heading to lunch. Are you free to come with me? I've been meaning to tell you, Raven, I've never seen you so happy. Love looks good on you." Her face heated up knowing why she was so happy. "Are you going to tell me when a baby is coming?"

"What?" Grandma sat back down. "I mean, what? You want to know when we're having a baby? I can tell you that when it happens. Not that it's happened yet. That would be preposterous. I mean, we've only just gotten married, how would I know — ?" Grandma shouted her name. "Grandma, don't tell anyone."

"You're going to have another baby?" The whisper wasn't all that low, nor would anyone call it inaudible. But Raven loved her, so forgave her for saying it so loudly. "Really? When did you find out?"

"You know that I'm a tiger, right?" Grandma nodded, scooting the chair ever closer to her desk. "Not only did Sawyer know that I was ovulating, but he also knows the exact minute that I conceive. I've not told anyone but you,

KATHI S. BARTON

so don't tell Dad yet. All right? We're going to wait until Thanksgiving."

"That's still two months away, Raven. You cannot expect me to keep quiet about this for that long. Please let me tell him." Raven told her no. "Please. I'd love to— Oh my goodness. You have to let me tell Merriam when the time comes. I promise not to tell your father if you let me break the news to Merriam. You know that she's not going to be happy. Not that I care, but she's not."

"We already told her just to piss her off, but I don't think she believed us. She's not happy with Sawyer and I now. And yesterday she made Molly cry." Grandma stiffened her back and asked her what had happened. "Molly was at the mall with Sippy picking out clothing and Mother caught up with them. She has been wanting to wear what she calls real people clothing to school since she figured out that other kids don't wear uniforms. Well, this school that she's going to now doesn't have much of a dress code. When she showed her grandma what she was going to wear on her first day, Mother ripped the shirt off of her and stomped on it. Had I been there, I would have done a great deal more than call for security. But Sippy said that she was just too angry to speak at that moment. Molly went to find Sawyer. You were at work and she wanted some arms around her, she told me."

"I dislike that woman more and more every day. What sort of shirt was it? I'll get her another one." Raven was glad to say that Sawyer had taken her shopping, and bought her several more of the shirt in different colors. "I love that man. I'm so very glad that he is taking care of my girls. You tell him that I love him for that."

Grandma left, upset about Molly and disappointed that

144

Raven couldn't have lunch with her. Grandma's lunches were not just lunch, Raven knew. They were lunch, shopping, snacks, a little shopping, then dinner. She loved her to pieces, but didn't have time for an all-day lunch. Raven would make it up to her soon, she promised herself.

By the time she was ready to leave for the day she'd gotten a lot done. Of course, it was never as much as she thought that she should have done, but making up for lost time was getting easier to cover. Sara brought in a file just as Raven was closing down her computers.

"Two things I need to run by you. Before that, however, the computer guy, Thomas, he's been working on the security cameras. Anyway, he's got them all up and running again, and there is no blipping in and out like before. I think I like him better than you right now." Raven said thanks. "Okay, two things. One, we need to upgrade our security system. I told him to go ahead and do whatever he needed, but he said that he wanted to hear it from the lady who had hired him. I said I'd have you call him. Second thing—you're not going to like this. Your mother is here. She's been in the lobby for the last twenty minutes waiting for you to be finished working so she can hit you on the way out. No excuses, she told the doorman."

"Damn it." Sara nodded. If anyone knew the true relationship between her and her mother, it was Sara. "I don't even have a plausible excuse either. Damn it again."

"If I were you, I'd introduce her to the staff at the door, then tell them that if she tries to enter again, they are to call the police. I wouldn't normally have someone call the police on their own mother, but she's been down there all this time, telling anyone that goes by her what a horrid person you are."

Raven was struck silent by that. "Also, she's been looking for Molly. I don't know why, but that's what she's asked several staff members."

"I'm finished with her." Standing up, she made her way to the door, Sara right behind her with her purse and coat. "Why wasn't I informed earlier of this?"

"They thought she was some nut ball that had wandered in to get warm. Which, when you see her, you'll understand. When was the last time that she had her hair done? My goodness Raven, she looks like it's been years." Raven told Sara that her dad had filed for divorce. "Well, that explains a lot. She's looking it. Being divorced, I mean."

Raven took the elevator down to the main floor. Several of the security staff were hanging around what she assumed was the chair her mother was in. Raven could hear her from where she was at the elevator, complaining about how Raven was the worst daughter in the world. She then went on about the bastard Addington.

Jerking the chair around, Raven was at first startled by her mother's appearance. But when Merriam spit at her, Raven not only got her speech back, but fury too. Slapping her mother in the face felt good and horrible at the same time.

"What do you mean coming here and talking about us like we're some sort of horrible beings? You are not welcome here." Mother stood up and drew back her hand. "You let that swing, Mother, and there will be so many men atop you you'll think that you are in a gang bang."

Several men snickered and Raven glared at them. That shut them up. She looked back at her mother. Her hair was a mess. The dress she had on was crumbled and marred with dirt. The purse that she had on her arm was broken at the

146

buckle.

"What has happened to you? You look like you've been sleeping in the streets." Her mother glared. "I don't know if you are aware of this, Mother, but I'm a grown assed woman, and you glaring at me has no effect. What has happened to you?"

"You and your father is what has happened to me. Where is that brat of yours?" Raven told her to keep her mouth shout about Molly. "Molly—what a common, stupid name. But then I guess that's about right for an illegitimate baby that has the rights to carry the Addington name, isn't it? You couldn't even be bothered to marry the man."

"Because he was married already, and then he died. And Molly is no longer an Addington. She's a Bishop, the same as I am. Sawyer adopted her." That shook Merriam to the core, Raven saw. It had to be about Molly, because Merriam knew that her and Sawyer had been married. "What do you want? I'm not going to talk to Dad. I'm not going to give you money, and I'm certainly not going to feel sorry for you. You've made your bed, now you have to lie it in."

"I'm an Addington, for Christ's sake." Raven told one of the men there to call the police. "You'd do that to your own flesh and blood? Call the police on your mother when I'm already suffering enough? My God, I wish that I'd done something about you, too, like the others, before your father found out."

"What did you just say to me?" Her mother lifted her chin up and repeated what she'd said. "You had abortions before I was born? How could you?"

"It was easy. I had money and a problem, and I got it taken care of. You weren't the last one either. Not that I was able to see a doctor about you soon enough." Then she reminded her of how she'd tried to get her to abort the brat too.

Raven staggered back from her mother. It felt as if she'd punched her in the face and the heart. As her mother stood there, going on about how she'd gotten rid of several children that she'd never wanted in the first place, Raven sat down on the floor. It was too much. She was only vaguely aware of her mother leaving.

Baby, what is it? She looked around for Sawyer, asking him where he was. *I'm at work, honey. What is it? I'm coming to you.*

Yes, please. And bring my dad with you. Mother was here. Sawyer assured her that he was coming. *She aborted them, Sawyer. All of the others. She got rid of them like they were nothing at all.*

She didn't have any idea if she was making sense or not, but she hurt too badly to think about each word. Her mother, her own mother, had denied her brothers and sisters. Tried to have Raven's own child lost to her. Getting up, she made her way to the ladies' room and threw up everything that she had on her stomach. Then she sat down on the floor and laid her head against the cold tile wall.

~*~

Roger held his little girl as he waited on Sawyer. He had no idea what the younger man was doing, and he wasn't sure that he wanted to know either, but his baby was hurting and he couldn't make her speak to him.

"Daddy?" He looked into her eyes—they were pain filled and teary. "She killed them all. Mother, she had abortions before and after I was born, and she doesn't even care."

He started to tell her that it couldn't be his wife. Merriam

148

knew how much he'd wanted children. But then Sara touched him on the arm and handed him a bottle of water. Her nod was all he needed to know that Raven had hit on something that he'd never been aware of.

"Honey, talk to me, baby. When did she tell you this? Today? Is that why you're so upset?" He looked around for Sawyer again and saw him talking to the police. "There's your husband, Raven. I'm going to get him over here, and I'm going to talk to your mother for a moment."

"No, don't leave me. She's gone, anyway." He assured Raven that he'd be fine, but she wouldn't let go of his arm. "Daddy, all my family, she took them from us. From both of us."

"Oh, honey, I had no idea. None at all." He felt his own heart break now that he'd come to terms with it. Not really terms, he thought, but things were starting to fall into place. The trips abroad where she hadn't wanted him to go. When she'd been too ill for him to touch her, to go to her club.

Sawyer came toward them and shook his head when he asked where Merriam was. He didn't know what she was up to now, but he was certainly going to have his attorney dig deeper into her life.

He'd only wanted to distance himself from her, just to be no longer married to her. He'd even said to his attorney that he'd pay her monthly, give her something to live on. But if what Raven had said was true, then he was going to leave her less than penniless.

Just this morning he'd had her clothing sent to the cleaners. Some of the things still had tags on them, but sent them along he had. To let her have something that she seemed to treasure more than she ever had him.

Pulling out his phone as Sawyer entered the bathroom to be with Raven, Roger phoned his attorney. After telling him where he was and what he'd found out, Hinshaw didn't say a word. Roger knew in that moment that he'd known about her deeds.

"I found out about her appointments yesterday. You were so keen on getting this over with that I didn't tell you. You talking about Molly and the fun that the two you had made me think you were doing what was right. But not so much now." Roger asked him what he'd found out so far. Also, how many he was sure of by now. "She was using the fact that you made all those donations to the hospital for them to keep it out of their books. But like most people doing unlawful things, they kept records, afraid that it would come back on them." He asked him again how many times. "So far I've uncovered ten before Raven was born. Four more after she was."

Fourteen children. He knew that they'd not have had that many children if she'd not done what she'd done. But that choice had been taken from him. Roger also knew that a woman's body was her own. His heart just didn't agree with that when, as her husband, she'd never spoken to him about not wanting any children.

"Dig as deeply as you can into her. All the clothing that I took to the clearers this morning? I want you to take them to Raven's shop. She knows how to deal with that crap better than anyone." Hinshaw laughed and said that he could do that. "Also, I want the entire house stripped of every stick of furniture, every hanger and curtain in the house removed. Every wall painted and the carpets cleaned. I want no trace of her when it's finished."

"There are some pieces that were your mother's. Holly

might want those back, do you think?" Roger said that he'd ask her. "If she doesn't, perhaps you can give them to Molly. Molly might not enjoy them now, but she could sell them off and keep the money if she wants."

"Molly will want them, if for no other reason that they belonged to her great grandma. Also, do me a favor, will you? The accounts that I set up; I want them closed as of today. I know that cards have gone out, but it won't matter anyway if there is no money in the bank." Hinshaw said that he could notify her. "I guess we can do that. I don't want to have anyone else's life upset over this."

Roger was making decisions in anger, and that was never good. But for now, at least, he was feeling pretty fucking good about everything. He asked how long it would take before he could see things starting to happen.

"The house will be started on today. I'm assuming you don't want any of that either." Roger said that he didn't. "All right, I'll have the house emptied today, as well as have them put aside any personal items they might encounter while they're emptying out things. I'm working on getting a letter written up now to have sent to her by courier. I know that she was staying at the hotel down the road from Raven, but I don't know if she'll be there now. I'm also canceling her memberships to all the clubs she was in. She won't have any medical insurance either after the end of the day."

Roger watched as Sawyer took Raven to the elevators. She was looking better than she had before, and he was glad for that. Going to tell them that he had things to do, Raven asked him if he'd bring Molly back when he had time.

"Molly isn't at my house." Raven nodded and said that she'd been there since yesterday. "No. I took her to my mom's this morning. Then Mom texted me and said that she watched her walk up to the door when she took her home a few minutes ago. Are you sure that—?"

Raven called home in a panic, and Curtis told her that no one at the house had seen or heard from Molly. Sawyer took off running, yelling for someone named Patterson to stop for a moment. Raven made her way across the room too when the full implications of what was going on hit Roger. Merriam had taken Molly at some point; he just knew it. Holy fuck, she'd kill her too, Roger thought.

They worked for nearly an hour before it was determined that Molly wasn't at home. Nor was she at the school where she'd be going to this fall. There wasn't much in the way of clothing missing—her coat that he'd bought her before leaving his house, and her cell phone. Christ, he hoped to hell that they found Merriam before he did. Roger was going to kill her himself when he found her.

They all met at Raven and Sawyer's home for a base of operations. The people there were working on the computer and phones they'd set up to find them. No matter how many times he told Raven that he was sorry, she would tell him they'd find her.

When someone put a heavy hand on his back, he turned to look at Gunner, the man he was slightly afraid of and in awe of. He wasn't any bigger than Sawyer's other brothers, but he was much larger in the form of muscles. Gunner asked to talk to him in private.

"I can find her, but you have to do me one favor before I can do that. I need to have something of your wife's. Something that she would have used a great deal." Roger told him that he'd just sent all her clothing to the dry cleaners.

"That wouldn't work anyway. People touch each other and leave behind parts of them, scents that would fuck with the scent. I'd rather have a makeup brush or a hairbrush. Lipstick usually works the best."

Roger knew there were hundreds of tubes of the nasty shit in her bathroom. Taking Gunner to his home, he rummaged around in the room and found several tubes for him. Asking for them all, Gunner took them from Roger.

"You can find them with that?" Gunner nodded as he stepped out on the back deck. "Won't the smell of it or something get in the way? And why do you need so many of them? In the event that you didn't understand, I'm a wreck in thinking that it's my fault that Merriam has Molly."

The shrill whistle made him cover his ears, but it was the sight of several white eyes staring at him from the darkness that had him backing away from Gunner. Before he could ask him what the hell all the dogs were doing there, Roger realized that they were wolves.

"You start over there and I'll start here. Just hold the tube with one of these gloves on and let each of them smell it for as long as they need to."

Roger pulled on the latex glove and did just what he was told to do. Some members of the wolf pack would smell it very quickly, getting the scent and taking off into the woods again. But there were few, younger ones, that would smell it for a while before disappearing in the darkness. When they were all gone, a large man came out of the woods and hugged Gunner, as men do that are masculine and heavy on the testosterone.

"This is the pack master of the wolf pack around here. He is also a brother of mine. Not by blood, but in other ways."

Roger didn't ask. He thought he'd live longer if he didn't. "They'll be looking everywhere for your wife. Then we can find Molly."

"Raven said that you took Molly's blood before leaving the other day. Will you use that link to find her?" He just shook his head. "I don't understand. Wasn't that the way it was supposed to work?"

"Yes, but Molly isn't conscious right now." He felt his knees weaken as the words sank in. "She's not dead, or I'd know that right now. But she'd not able to respond to me because she's out cold. That doesn't mean dead, all right? Christ, humans are so easily scared about shit."

"She's my only grandchild, and I can appreciate you being all mean and macho, but she's the best thing since my daughter was born that I've ever loved. So, back the fuck off and deal with me being a human."

The big man, the pack leader, laughed, and Gunner turned to him.

"He's a good man. Not afraid of you as much as you think." The man came forward and put out his hand. "My name is Bob Smith. Crazy, I know, but all the cool names were taken when I was born."

Roger couldn't help it, he laughed. He thought it might have been the first one he'd had in his entire adult life. Hugging both men, he made his way back to Raven's home. To wait it out, he thought, however long it took.

Chapter 11

Merriam checked on the brat again. She had no use for children at all. They dated you if you took them anyplace with you. Like having a daughter old enough to have one of her own. That hadn't set well with Merriam since she'd found out that the abortion process to get rid of Raven hadn't worked.

The older Raven had gotten, the harder it was for Merriam to lie to people about her age. She'd been able to pull it off too, right up until Raven had gotten her driver's license, and that had been it for her telling people that she was ten to fifteen years younger than she actually was. Not even Roger knew her true age. She'd kept that from him as well.

Merriam supposed that she might have hit the kid too hard when the little kid didn't want to come with her. Then when she'd gotten her into the car, it had occurred to her that she was getting blood all over the seat. Damn it, she knew little to nothing about kidnapping, and here she was making a mistake that even she knew not to do.

Stealing the car wasn't difficult. When she'd been younger,

before becoming an Addington, she used to steal regularly when she needed a ride someplace. Her parents would never allow her to hitchhike, so she stole cars. Or she would borrow them, and leave them in pretty good shape when she was finished.

There were a great many things about her that her dear family didn't know. She supposed that was why she took being an Addington so seriously. She'd grown up being just plain old Janet Stipple, without any shoes in the summer months like the other kids had. If she hadn't outgrown the ones that she'd gotten in the new school year, then she could put those on. But usually, one of her brothers or sisters would need them for winter. And with having two older sisters, there was never anything new for her. Six sisters and four brothers had made life hard for her. No one understood her need to have more than most anyone else she knew.

Then there had been the fire. She'd set it, of course. Merriam had thought that if she'd thought of it sooner, she would have done it then. Things had become very different for her once she was put into the system as an adoptable little girl. Merriam smiled when she thought of how much work and effort she'd put in when someone came to look over the kids at the home.

After four years she was considered as unadoptable. She'd had her fair share of families to take her home, but they all brought her back. The rules that they'd had made her a target with the other children. Then came the Tractors.

They were an older couple—in their early forties, she supposed. They'd had plenty of money, and they didn't seem to care what she did so long as she was dressed well for dinner, didn't give them too much trouble, and was able to be polite when they had her around other people. That hadn't been any problem for her.

Merriam had changed her name when she was adopted. Pretending that the fire that took her entire family was such a nightmare for her had the judge eating out of her hands. By the time the adoption was finalized, Merriam had a new name, a new life, and knew that so long as she could keep out of serious trouble, she'd have three meals a day, as well as a roof over her head when it rained.

Looking at Molly the brat again, Merriam wondered how long she'd been awake. As she sat in the chair, tied up and gagged, Merriam did have a moment of fear when she looked like she wasn't afraid at all. Taking the gag off her so she could make a few things clear to the kid, Merriam slapped her, just because she could.

"You'll be talking to your mother for me." Nothing. Not even a small whimper of pain for the slap. "And you'll tell her that I want to go back to my way of life. That I'm sorry about the other kids. Any kind of bullshit that you can think of, you use it to get me back to my life. Did you hear me?"

"Yes. But it's not going to work. Grandpa Roger said that he's happier without you around." She hit her again, this time knocking the chair back. Merriam could hear her head hit the floor, and was sort of happy that she'd hurt her twice with one blow. "They'll be coming for me, and there won't be any way of stopping them from hurting you once they get here."

Merriam didn't care for the fact that Molly was acting all brave and stuff. She even left the brat on the floor, hoping that would shut her up. But so far all it had done was made her mouthier, and that was something that Merriam didn't care for.

Hitting her again while she was down made Merriam happy that she'd worn her nice tall heels when she'd left the house that morning. When nothing more was coming from the kid, Merriam went to the bathroom to see if she'd messed up her hair or nails. Everything about her screamed money now that she'd gone to her regular hairdresser. Getting her to accept the excuse of forgetting her purse didn't go over as well as she'd hoped, however.

Another two people that she'd had to kill in the name of being an Addington. Kian, her tranny hairdresser, had objected right away to the plan of Roger coming by with money. Lily, the lady that did her nails, said that she could wait, but she was going to get a bigger tip. When Kian picked up the phone to make sure she was good for the money, Merriam took one of the teasing combs they'd used on her and stabbed her right in the neck. Lily, a fat older woman, was a piece of cake after that.

The new dress had come from the same shop. Kian would purchase used clothing, have it dry cleaned, and resell it. Low and behold, there were two of her castoffs in the place, and Merriam took both of them. Also a purse. But the heels were just too low for her, so she'd had to clean her heels up and wear those.

Now here she was with all the makeup that she could stuff into a bag and another clean dress to wear. Merriam knew that once she was ready to go back to her home, she'd be throwing out everything and starting new. And just so no one else could take her clothing and wear them, she was going to have them cut up into small pieces. No one would be able to imitate her ever again.

The money from the drawer and tip jar hadn't been as

much as she wanted, not with everyone paying in credit cards now, but it was enough to have a good meal with and to flash around the club. It was very nice of Roger to have paid for her to have her memberships back. She only hoped that Raven and her new husband didn't have one there too.

"That would be just too much for me to handle right now."

Checking on Molly again, Merriam noticed the blood staining the floor. She didn't want her to die just yet — that would be for later. She did think that it looked like a red melted candle. A memory came to her head, but it was gone before she could think about it. Merriam put a towel over the stain and left the vacant building.

Merriam moved out of the building and toward where she'd parked the car. It was missing. She was sure that she'd parked it by the front of the building so she could get out fast if she had to. Looking around, trying to get her bearings, she finally realized that she'd not come out the way she'd gone in. That, her mother would have said, was a bad omen.

Her mother had had a lot of old sayings of crap like that. Don't go in a door that you didn't leave. Never spill salt in the morning or you'll have a nasty visitor. The one that Merriam thought was the most stupid was don't sit in the grass or you'd get a cold where you can't take medications.

"Like you could catch a cold in your butt. Stupid woman."

Running her hand over the nice car, she wished that she could have found herself a driver. Not that she didn't enjoy driving — she really did — but the club would make her park in the lot then walk across the parking lot to the building. She thought that with a name like Addington and how much she spent there, every week they'd make sure she had her own parking space.

Driving to the country club, she thought of little else but living in her home again. Driving by the hair salon, she saw that the police were there, as well as a bunch of men that were just milling around sniffing the air. Whatever that was about made her giggle.

Her home was on the next block, so she went there. But there was trouble there too. A line of cruisers with their lights on were parked on her lawn and driveway. She made a mental note to call the mayor of their fine city and have him pay for a sod replacement.

If Merriam wasn't worried about her clothing and her name, she worried about the way her house looked. Picture perfect all the time was what she wanted, and the gardeners were well aware of what happened to them if it had one bush shorter or taller than the others.

She was just driving by her home when she felt something knock her head from behind. It didn't really hurt, and after a moment, she didn't even think of it again. Looking around, Merriam had trouble making out the street signs, as well as whether or not the lights were green or red. Wiping her head with her gloved hand, she felt slightly sick to her stomach, but chalked that up to all the stress she'd been under lately.

The club was hopping tonight. She only just remembered that it was fish fry Friday. Not that she cared for the foul smelling fish, but she did enjoy seeing all her friends there as they came to gorge on deep fried fish and coleslaw. They all looked at her too, she thought, vying for her attention like she was queen of the roost. Merriam would always have a new outfit on, and made sure that the reflection of the diamonds in her rings could dance off the ceiling if someone wasn't paying her the due that she deserved.

When this nonsense was all finished with Roger and Raven, she was going to see if she could run for president of the club. She would no doubt win, but she'd have to have a platform to run off of. She had thought of this before, and had written down a few things that she wanted to get changed. Like no children should ever be allow in the place without handcuffs on their filthy little hands and their mouth covered in tape.

Pulling into the closest parking space that she could find, Merriam repaired her lipstick and made sure that she had her membership card ready. That was another thing she'd change. Carrying around a card when you were there almost daily seemed unimportant. She'd make sure there were other means of getting in the place. More secure, she thought.

Getting out of her car, she held onto the door handle. Her head was swimming a little, and she wasn't sure when it had started raining. The back of her dress was going to be ruined if she didn't get inside soon.

There was a new man at the door. Winking at him as he allowed her entrance, Merriam wondered if she could get a little bit of him when she left. While she never wanted another child, she certainly did like her sex. Random sex, not with the same boring ass every night.

Entering the dining room where the dinner was going on, she paused in the doorway when she noticed that no one was in there eating. Sitting at her usual spot, Merriam asked the waitress who brought her a glass of water and a glass of wine where everyone was. There must have been a big meeting, she thought, and she'd missed the letter. When the girl didn't answer her, Merriam asked if she was deaf.

"No, ma'am. I can hear you just fine." Merriam asked again where everyone was. "They're here. Everyone is here. We're really busy tonight. Do you just want the special?"

Merriam looked around at the empty tables. There were plates and drink glasses on each of them. Napkins were on the chairs, but there wasn't a single person in the room except the dummy taking her order and herself. She asked her again if she wanted the special.

"I do not eat that greasy stuff. I want a Porterhouse steak, rare, baked potato, as well as a cup of the soup of the day. It's tomato basil, correct?" The dummy told her that they didn't have any potatoes as they'd run out, and the soup was what it always was on Friday nights, Manhattan chowder. "No, that's not right. I know better than anyone what sort of meals they serve here. I've been a member for longer than you've been alive. Not too much longer—I'm not that old—but a while now."

"I'm sorry, ma'am." Dummy stared at her for a moment and asked if she was all right. "You're bleeding from your head. Want me to get you some ice for it?"

She was? Merriam waved the waitress away and pulled out her compact. There was blood on her head. It was running down not just her forehead, but her cheek as well. Wiping at it with her napkin, Merriam stuck the end of the fine linen into her water and tried to clean herself up. It was doing her very little good.

A man, a huge great man, sat down at the table with her. He took her wine glass from her table and drained it in one drink. She wanted to say something to him, demand that he replace her drink, when he stretched out on his chair and she could see that he was a very good looking male.

"What are you going to do to replace my drink, big boy?"

He laughed, and it sounded sexy to her. Looking around the room again when he waved at the table next to them, she asked him what his name was.

"Gunner." She loved the way he said it too. like he was grunting his name for her. "You've not been a very good person, have you, Janet Stipple? In fact, I can say for a fact that you've been downright nasty."

She liked the sound of that too.

~*~

Raven didn't want to go in and sit with her mom. Nor did she want to sit calmly by her and pretend like nothing had happened over the last twenty-four hours. Gunner had found her when no one else could, and she would be forever grateful to him. If only someone could find her Molly, then her life would be perfect.

"What the hell are you doing here? Of all the tables in this place that are empty, why the hell are you sitting with me?" Raven looked around at the crowd of people in the room, then back at her mother when she laughed. "I don't know what's going on here, but apparently they want me to believe that there are hundreds of people in here instead of just the three of us. But I am so glad that you've come to visit me. I thought that you'd died that night."

Raven had been told three times not to ask about her daughter. There were people out looking for her. Gunner left them and headed around the tables when she looked to her mother. There was blood all over her face and hands, and Raven wondered if it was her mother's or Molly's. She hoped for her mother's sake that it was hers and not her daughter's.

Raven, honey, Gunner is going to get Molly. He said that he knows just where she is. Has she said anything about the blood? The cop that shot at her said that he thought he only broke a window. Perhaps he did more than that. Ask her about it.

Raven looked at her mother and asked her if she'd been hurt.

"No. You're the second person that's asked me that. I'm perfectly fine, Rachel." Rachel? Raven asked her who that was, remembering that she'd had a sister of that name. But she had died long ago. "You, you dummy. You're my sister Rachel. Don't be stupid, and tell me what you're doing here. How did you escape the fire?"

Raven knew about the fire too. There had been one when her mother was just a little girl, and it had taken the life of her entire family. What no one still knew was what had caused it and how Janet had gotten out. To find out that her mother was this entirely different person had blown her away.

Raven looked to where the others were sitting. "I've no idea how I got out of the fire, Janet. I must have been with you." Her mother shook her head, and said that she'd been hiding out in the barn. The fire hadn't caught there yet. "I don't know then. Do you know how the fire was set? Some are thinking that you did it. Did you? That would be so cool if you did." Sawyer asked her what she was doing. *I don't know. But let me just figure this out, all right?*

"Wasn't me. I did think about it a lot. I mean, there were so many candles in the place, all it would take was for one of them to be knocked over." Mother leaned closer to her, still talking to her liked she was her sister, Rachel. "I mean, there wasn't any way that I put a nice fat candle on the cast iron heater and let it melt all over the place before I left. No siree, wasn't me."

The laughter sounded manic. Insane. This wasn't her mother, she had to keep telling herself. This was a person who had just admitted that she'd killed her family. All of them. But for what reason?

"What have you been doing with yourself? I mean, I wouldn't have known you without your...your hair color." Janet laughed again at Raven's question, and Raven felt a little more of her heart break for who she had thought was just mean. No, this woman was a murderer. "You live around here?"

"I used to." The frown made Raven think that she hurt to remember her or her father. Changing the subject, she thought about the things she'd read in the hastily written report that Gunner had found. "Where have you been all this time?"

"Here and there. I have a daughter now." That made her head hurt, Raven saw. With her fingers to her temple, Janet was spreading blood around her face more. "Did you have a home to go to when you left the burning house?"

"Oh yes. I had a lot of them. Of course, none of them could handle me. I was such a wild child back then. I mean, they had all these rules. Just like Mom and Dad did. Don't do this, don't take the grocery money. I wasn't allowed to steal magazines off the racks. That one really bothered me. How was I supposed to make myself look like I was above all of them when I didn't know what good looking people looked like? You look just like you did as a kid, Rachel. Pretty hair. Nice full lips. I hated that you were pretty and didn't have to do anything to make boys like you."

"Is that why you set the fire? To kill me off because I was pretty?" Janet nodded, and said that Maggie was getting to be too pretty for her too. "Maggie, our little sister. You didn't

165

like that she was pretty too?"

"Hell no. I decided right then and there I was never going to have any kids that would be prettier than me." She looked at her, and Raven had a feeling that she was trying very hard to figure out who she really was. "Rachel?"

"Yes." Raven waited. She wanted to find out more, find more out about her mother that she'd never know. "What about Samuel? I mean, he was your...our brother. He couldn't be prettier than you were, could he?"

"No, I guess not. But I had to get away from all of them. They were like leeches. Wanting to know what I was doing all day. Trying to get me to do housework and shit. I hated that kind of stuff. When I grew up, I knew that I was going to be someone that took pride in everything I had. Show it to the world that I had it all." Janet frowned again. "Did I get that? Money and stuff?"

"Yes. You had lots of it." Janet laid her head on the table. "Are you all right? Is there something that I can do for you?"

"No, I don't want anything from anyone, Rachel. If you continue to be alive, I'm going to have to kill you—you know that, don't you? I mean, you're very beautiful, but I need to be the one that people admire." She picked up the knife and Raven took it from her. "If I don't kill you now, I know that I won't get the chance again. Right?"

"You don't want to kill me, Janet. You can't." She asked her why not. "Because I'm not your long dead sister that you killed. I'm your daughter. Raven."

With her head still on the table, Janet/Mother looked at her. She didn't say anything, but Raven could see that blood was pooling under her head. She knew that she might be dying, and hated that she really didn't care right now.

Raven looked at Sawyer when he sat down at the table with them.

"Molly is in the hospital. She has head trauma, but Gunner has made sure that she'll be just fine." She asked him if he'd converted her. "No. He didn't say that it would be necessary, but he won't do it. You and I will have to if it comes to that. I've called an ambulance."

"She killed her family because they were prettier than her." He nodded, and Raven looked at her mother, who now had her eyes closed. "I feel so ashamed right now. I don't care if she lives or dies. She's hurt so many people in her life."

"Yes, but will you be able to live with yourself if you think on it later and realize that you were the one that let her die?" She shook her head. "Take the knife there and cut a small wound into your thumb. Put your blood onto her tongue, and it should be enough to slow the bleeding down. You can hear her heart beating too, so you know that it's getting weaker."

"I can hear it." Doing what Sawyer suggested, she put her blood on her mother's tongue. Startled by the look that her mother gave her, Raven gave her just a little more. "I just realized that I don't want her to die. I want her to pay for all the things that she's done. Not just to me, but to everyone that she's killed. They deserve some peace, not her."

"When you're ready, we'll go to the hospital. She'll be fine here. Your dad is coming to be with her until she gets to the hospital." Getting up, Raven looked at her mother once more, unsure why all of a sudden she felt sorry for her. "Raven, she doesn't deserve you. She's nothing to you now."

"I'm not sure that she ever was. A murderer? Yes. Thief? Yes. But my mother? Grandmother to my children? Never."

She moved out of the club just as the ambulance was

167

pulling up. Raven knew that she must look frightful. There was blood all over her hands and dress that she had on. When they got to the car, Sawyer handed her a bag and she changed into some pants and a T-shirt. Cleaning up with the wipes that were in the car too, she thought about her new life.

"I love you, Sawyer. I'm so glad that you saved my life twice." He asked her what she meant. "When you saved my life at the beating, and today when you made me realize that I don't have to love or respect someone just because I'm supposed to. Mother never did anything for me other than to just make me hate her."

"She made you into what you are, regardless of what she did to make you that way. And for that, I will thank her. But nothing else." He took her hand into his. "I love you very much too, Raven. And will for the rest of our days together."

Chapter 12

They drove to the hospital and Raven ran in ahead of him to see Molly. Parking the car, he made his way into the curtained off area that he'd been told Molly was in. His brother hugged him, and quietly told him what he'd found when he got to the vacant building.

"She had been tied to a chair. I'm going to teach her how to get out of one when she's better. At some point, I can only assume she hit Molly and the chair fell over. It looks as if Merriam had also kicked Molly several times with her high heels." Sawyer asked about the head wound. "They've stitched her up after doing x-rays. Fourteen stitches. But they're worried because she lost a great deal of blood. I've not given her any. I was waiting to see what you would like to do."

"I'll give her what I can." Sawyer looked at his brother when Raven spoke. She turned to look at them. "What are you trying very hard not to tell me?"

"I'd rather you didn't." She stood up, ready to do battle

with him. "Let me explain. When you gave your mother that little bit of extra, it was more than I thought you should have." Then through their link, so Gunner couldn't hear, he told her, *You have to think of the baby now.* "I'm not saying that you can't give her any of yours, but you will need to make sure that it's only a few drops. Just until we are sure that there won't be any trouble after she wakes up." Sawyer finished up so that Gunner could hear why he didn't want Raven to give her much.

"I guess I can understand that." Raven looked back at Molly. "Will it do anything to her? I mean, can she talk to me like you two can?"

"Yes. It might even give her a little magic. But we won't know what that might be until she discovers it herself." Raven asked if that would be a bad thing. "Not necessarily. But if she discovers it around others, humans, it might not settle well with them. You'll have to have a talk with her when she wakes up."

"So long as she wakes up, I don't care if she can make bubbles out her ass." Both he and Gunner laughed. Raven smiled. "I guess that was a stupid comment. But when can we do this? Now is fine by me."

"Yes, so long as we're careful with it. I know that it seems silly to worry about a few drops of blood from you, but you gave your mother a lot, and I need to keep you healthy for us, so you'll—"

"Sawyer, honey, I don't suppose you can do this later—after we save our daughter? I want her to wake up and speak to me. All right?" He smiled at her and bit down on his thumb. "I suppose you had me use a knife before because you didn't want me to freak out. I am, just so you know."

"I love you, Raven Bishop. Now hush and let me save our little girl." His blood was stronger than Raven's. He was full blooded, and she was only just turned. Sawyer didn't really need her to give any of her blood, but he wanted her to feel like she helped. He thought that she might need that as much as anything right now. "Okay, just a few drops, Raven, all right?"

She counted them as she dropped them onto Molly's tongue. He watched her as she held her thumb over her daughter's mouth, and when she pulled away without risking her life and that of their child, he let go of the breath he'd been holding.

Gunner left when Molly was being transported to a room. Holly showed up a few minutes later, sobbing and crying about her little baby. Over and over, she kept telling Molly how sorry she was. No matter how many times Raven told her that it wasn't her fault, she just didn't believe them.

It was well after midnight when Roger joined them. Sawyer said that he was going to stretch his legs, and Roger, after kissing all three of the women, asked if he could go too. There was a sadness about him that broke Sawyer's heart.

"Merriam is going to live. The doctors are baffled as to how she could have lived as long as she had and made it to the hospital. I'm assuming that you had something to do with that." He told her that Raven had done it. "Why? As much as I love my daughter, I hate Merriam all that much and more. Why would she want her to be saved?"

"She killed her family. Burnt the house down around them while she was hiding in the barn. She also killed a hairdresser and a nail person. Robbed the place of not just money from the drawer, but also their purses. Merriam took a few things from the store, too, but it's petty after she killed them both."

"That doesn't answer the question as to why Raven would save her mother." Sawyer told Roger what Raven had said. "Oh. I guess I never thought about closure for anyone else but myself. I can't believe the things that I'm finding out about her. None of it came out when I did a background check on her, simply because I didn't have her real name. You know, I only married her because I wanted children, and she seemed to want them as well. Of all the things I've done in my lifetime, that's the one thing that I'll regret most."

"You shouldn't, Roger." He asked him why the fuck not. "Without Merriam, you never would have had Raven or Molly. And even though Raven wants to tell you later, we're going to have another child sometime in the early summer of next year."

"No." Sawyer nodded. "Really? Another grandchild? I will do better with this one. On that I've already made a promise to myself—assuming, I guess, that the two of you would want a child of your own."

"Molly is just as much my child as Raven is yours. I love her with all my heart." Roger hugged him, sobbing about the mistakes that he'd made while he leaned heavily on him. "You're going to be just fine. And before I forget, I know that you're having your home redone—great idea, I think. Anyway, Raven and I would like it very much if you came to live with us while it's going on. Perhaps after it's done you'll feel so good about being around that you'll just stay there."

"I don't think that— Hell, I'm not going to lie to you, I'd love to be out of that house. Maybe I can convince someone in your family to take it off my hands." Sawyer laughed, sure that he was just joking. "Yes, I'd love to live with you and your family. I think it would do me a great deal of good with my whole starting my life over project."

"Great. So, when Raven tells you, you'll act surprised, won't you? I mean, she might not want to hang around with me either if she finds out." Roger said he could do that as well. They went to the cafeteria to get some drinks before going up to the room.

Sawyer's parents had shown up while he and Roger were outside. His mother hugged him several times before she let his dad hug him. They both sat by the bed with Raven and touched Molly, telling her all the things they were going to do with her when summer rolled around again.

"Holly—I can call you that, can't I?" Holly told Sippy that she'd like that very much. "I want to tell you something. You can relate to it, I think. When Sawyer was just a young boy, about Molly's age or so, I dropped him off at school. I was in a hurry to run some errands and didn't bother to see if he made it into the building or not. On my way home I was surprised to see how many other children were out playing in their yards. That was when I spied my son. He was in the yard of one of the other children, helping Mr. Abbot rake up his leaves. As you can imagine, I was so mad at him. Skipping school was not something that I would allow the children to do."

"It was a weekend, wasn't it? I've done that before with Roger." Mom shook her head. "Okay, what happened?"

"There was a bomb threat. Not a threat, I suppose, but a real bomb. One of the children had brought it in for a science project. He didn't know that it was real, but put it in his locker to take to class later. The heat of the day made it go off." Holly asked if anyone had been hurt. Mom looked at him to continue the story.

"I could hear it. Also, I could smell the gun powder. So when I guessed what it was, I pulled the fire alarm. Just as everyone was able to get out of the school, the bomb, a nice sized one, went off and blew out two walls in the building. One of them being the assembly room that we were all in for a pep rally." Holly asked him if he'd been in trouble. "No. Mom and Dad were the only ones that knew what I'd done. There weren't any cameras in the building back then, so there was no footage of me pulling the fire alarm. The school just figured that the heat of the day had done it, or some higher power. Whatever they believed, I let them. It was better than having to explain how I had heard the ticking of the bomb or was able to smell gun powder."

"Oh my. I don't know what to say. You saved all those lives." Mom said that Holly was missing the point. "No, I don't think so. Although I don't know what this has to do with me leaving Molly alone so that she could be taken by Merriam."

"It has everything to do with it. You see, I would never have become a cop if I'd not done what I did that day. Not just saving the others, but being able to figure things out. I put it together, like I do cases that I'm working on. I've been able to close a great many cases because of that one day. Also saved a lot of lives. The same with what happened today." Holly looked at him, confused. "I know you feel guilty about dropping off Molly. But with her being taken, you were able to find out just what sort of person Merriam is. If not, the police would never have been able to figure out how an entire family had been killed with only one survivor. Yes, people were killed, but in the long run, you can only guess how many more would have died at her hand. But the most important thing is, Molly is going to live. She has powerful blood in her system that will keep her alive for a long time, not to mention let her heal much faster. And she will more than likely never get ill again. Plus, there is no telling what she'll do with the events of the day. It's all up to her. She's alive. That's all you should be focusing on."

Sawyer hoped that he got through to Holly. He didn't want her dwelling on things that could never be changed. They were all alive, safe, and together. That's what his mom had told him the day after the explosion. That she was just grateful that they were still a family. He had never forgotten that since she'd told him.

The sun was coming up when Sawyer thought that he could sleep standing up. It had been a hell of a twenty-four hours, and he wasn't sure how much longer he could go. Just as he was leaning back in the chair that had been brought in for the others, he heard Molly say "Dad."

Looking at her, he asked her if she was all right through their link. Excitement was all over her face then, and she answered him back the same way. He was so happy to see her that he had to hold back his own tears.

Yes. I have a bit of a headache, but I'm okay. Did you make me into a tiger too? He said that he'd not had to, her head was harder than any of them had noticed. *Very funny. But I do feel different. Could it be just the headache?*

It could be. He wouldn't tell her until her mother was awake. He figured that she'd try out everything that she could think about just to see if she had any magic. *You should wake your mom. She's been waiting for you to wake up and give her a hug.*

175

I love you, Dad. I've never said that before to anyone except Mom and GGma, but I do love you. He said that he loved her too. *I'd like to see your tigers, yours and Mom's. If that's okay?*

It is. He'd like to meet you too. *He's a big guy, bigger than the ones in the zoo, and he'll be bigger than your mom's too.* She asked him if he was always going to protect her. *Forever. Forever and a day.*

~*~

Raven listened to the man on the other end of the phone going on and on about his order. He wanted it shipped to him in separate boxes, so that he'd not have to find a box to wrap it in. He wanted it to arrive day after tomorrow, all shipped to the same address. And oh, remember, he told her, he was to get free shipping because he ordered enough in gifts to qualify for it.

"I can do that for you, sir. However, I won't be able to ship it so that it arrives the day after tomorrow. That would be more in shipping for it to go next day air." He started to tell her that it said free shipping. "It says free standard shipping. I can ship it out to you for free, but it won't arrive at your home for ten business days or more."

Rolling her eyes when Sara came into her office, she listened to the man talk about suing her. As much as she wanted to hang up on him, she knew that it would be just what he wanted in order to give her store a bad rating. Instead, she asked him if he wanted it to go out standard mail.

"I do not. I want the packages to arrive day after tomorrow, and I want it to be free. You either play ball or I'm going to go over your head and speak to the manager." She told him that she was the owner of the company. He hung up on her. Raven asked Sara what she needed.

"Nothing much. I just needed to get away from the new guy, Josh. He's a talker, isn't he?" Raven said that she nearly couldn't get off the phone with him when she'd called in yesterday. "Yes, well, I have to terminate him anyway. He failed his drug test this morning. Also, and here is the real kicker, he told the personnel that took the test that he's been doing some coke to keep him on his level. Whatever the hell that means."

Raven asked Sara if she wanted to do it or if she should. Sara said no, she would do it. Just as she was leaving, her phone rang and Sara answered it. Handing it to her with a huge smile, she left the room, closing the door behind her.

"Hello, my beautiful wife." She smiled and asked Sawyer if he was having a good day. "I am, as a matter of fact. I don't think the three people I just fired are, but I am."

She told him about the man and his free shipping. "I don't mean to sound dense, but what is it you do there? I mean, I know you're the boss, but what is it your company does? I should know this, I know, but we've not exactly had a very slow start to our marriage so far."

"I sell high end used clothing. All shapes and sizes. I hit on it when I was looking for a prom dress when I was in high school. They were going for hundreds of dollars, and while I could afford it, I thought that it was stupid to pay seven hundred bucks for a dress that I would probably wear only the one time." He called her practical. "Mostly, I guess. So the day after prom, I bought up every dress I could find. There were a great many of them too, and for nearly nothing. I did that for about four years, until I was twenty something and could open my own store. Then it just took off."

"I bet. And now you sell a lot more than that, right?"

She said that she did. "Sometimes, a lot of the times, a company will call me up and ask me to buy out something that didn't go over too well in the market. I get it for nearly nothing compared to what they were selling it for. So I just remarket them and sell them. It's been a great money maker for a long time."

"And the stuff that doesn't sell, what do you do with that?" She told him that she donated it to the local shelters, who use it for job interviews and such. "That's a wonderful service you have there. I bet wedding dresses are big too."

"You have no idea. I would bet that nearly a quarter of my inventory is wedding dresses. Also, they sell the most too. People are in for a great bargain with that sort of thing. Bridesmaids dresses are also a huge seller." She asked him why he called. "I do have a job here, you know."

"Yes, and you're very good at it. I'm stalling." She asked him why he was doing that. "I sort of did something without asking you. I don't think you'll be mad at me, but with you— well, I've not learned all your anger spots yet."

"Tell me. Whatever it is, I might only beat you up a little bit. And if it's like the time you asked my father to come and live with us—which I love, by the way—that won't be bad at all." He said that it was bigger than that. "Oh my. I am curious now."

"The school needed a new gymnasium. The one that they had for the last twenty some odd years has been deemed unusable. Not just the floor, but the bleachers as well as the basketball hoops. This morning, one of the employees here was playing ball before the bell rang, and one of the floorboards came up and cut him pretty badly. He's going to be just fine— he's a wolf—but he was hurt, and that brought in the police who brought in some inspectors. I told them that we'd have it renovated." She didn't see anything wrong with that, but before she could answer, he continued. "It just so happened that your dad and grandma were there, and they're going to go in thirds with us. The district doesn't have the money. I'm sorry, honey."

"Why?" He told her that even at a third of the cost it was going to be a great deal of money. "Sawyer, it's great that you did it. I would have too, and would have been pissed off that Grandma and Dad helped out and we didn't. They're good at finding out what we're doing when it comes to helping out the city."

"Your dad said you'd not be mad, but I didn't know for sure." Raven told him never about things like that. "I told my brothers that they had to help with the construction and demolition of the gym. They were all for it. And since my dad is feeling so much better, he said he'd help too."

"A family effort. I love it." Leaning back in her chair, she asked him how things were going there, other than the firing of someone. "We're gearing up for the holidays here. I had four hundred Santa suits, but we sold them almost as soon as they were put online."

"Roger came in with my mom and dad, and they're going to have lunch with me. Just the four of us, he said. We have to talk, I was told. Do you suppose your dad wants me to take care of an old girlfriend? As a matter of fact, do you think your dad will ever date again?" Laughing at him, she told him no, she didn't think so. "I think it would be good for him, to see that not all women would be like your mother was to him. It might be something he could do to have a friend too."

"I don't know, actually. It could be just that they want to

179

know what you want to do about Christmas or something."
He asked if she knew that or was guessing. Sawyer was
sounding very happy now. "I guess you'll have to go to lunch
with them and find out, now won't you?"

After talking about dinner plans they hung up. Getting
back to work, she was nearly finished with the marketing of
maternity shirts that she'd gotten in when Sara came back in.
She looked to be very happy about something.

"Mr. Harper called back in. He's the one that wanted free
next day shipping on his order." Raven asked if he'd gotten
it. "No, but he told them that you said it would be just fine for
them to do this, one time."

"I hope no one fell for that." Sara shook her head. "What
does he want now, for us to ship it so that it gets there today?"

"No." She started laughing. "You're not going to believe
this one. He said that he'd pay for the next day shipping if
we were to help him out by adding some pretty wrapping
paper—in a separate box, of course. Along with ribbons and
bows. Not that cheap shit, either."

"Is he aware that it's going to cost him about six hundred
dollars that way?" Sara laughed and said she wasn't finished
yet. "Oh no. This had better make my day. I really need it."

"Oh, it will. When the order was put in, with the next day
shipping, I was with the customer service rep. The CSR told
him what the amount was for the clothing that he was getting,
then the shipping. I could hear him screaming through the
headset, Raven. It was the funniest thing I've ever heard. He
screamed about how he'd not paid that much for the gifts,
and he certainly wasn't going to pay out the ass, his words,
to have it there tomorrow. You owe this CSR a brownie or
something. After the man calmed down, he told him that

he could have it there well before Christmas if he just took advantage of the free shipping. He even said that he'd go and get some pretty paper and ribbons to go out too."

"The stuff we have in storage for decorations?" Sara asked if that was all right. "Of course. Especially if the customer was happy with it."

"He is very happy. In fact, he asked for the CSR's name and said that he was going to personally write a letter to the owner of the company and make sure that she knew there were good employees working there. Unlike the person who said she was the owner."

Raven said she'd love that, not even upset that the man thought she'd lied to him. "Give me the CSR's name and I'll see that he gets a bonus of some kind. We should have a contest running again. It's been a while. How about we get on that? I don't care what we do, but the prizes will be gift cards."

"Speaking of which, the gift cards for Christmas are in. That's very generous of you, giving out that much for each person that works here." Raven said she'd not have a job if not for them. "I know. I think you're awesome."

After she left her for the second time, Raven pulled out her Christmas list. She was excited to go shopping this year. And with Molly and Grandma gone on their cruise right now, she knew that she could get things in without Molly ever knowing. Raven was so happy to have her daughter feeling better.

The day after Molly had been released from the hospital, they'd taken her out to the back yard and shifted for her. It had been Raven's first time in shifting from woman to cat, and she thought that she'd done a good job of it.

Her cat seemed to know that she was carrying a child. Raven hadn't put it together that her and her cat were actually two different beings. They didn't speak to each other, but they did communicate in other ways. Also, her cat seemed to know that Molly was still very tender about her wounds, as well as what her grandmother had done to her.

Molly was delighted with the cats. So was Raven. She jumped around the yard and stretched out in the grass for hours after Molly went inside. Then Sawyer showed her how cats had sex. While not as fulfilling as with him as a human, it was fun.

Raven was ready to go by four that night. No longer staying late to get just one more thing finished up, she was getting home in time to not just have dinner with her family, but also to sit around with Sawyer and read the paper. A thing that she'd never been able to do before. It was her own fault, but she was glad for the change of it.

Her dad and Sawyer were in the back, working on putting the grill together. She'd had one when Sawyer moved in, but it had been too old to make work. Raven had only bought it because Molly had wanted a hotdog on the grill for dinner one night. And Raven being Raven, she had to read all the instructions to it before she used it. Molly got bored waiting, and they ended up with pizza instead. Raven gave Sawyer a kiss, then her father, and noticed that he had a black eye. Asking him about it, he told her that it was nothing and didn't want to talk about it. Looking at Sawyer for an answer, he just shook his head.

He went to see your mother today. She wasn't happy that he was there and not letting her get back in their home or out of police custody. I think he was more upset that he allowed her to hit him than that she actually did. I believe that he's finally come to terms with the fact that she is a horrible person. Raven asked if he was all right. *Yes, just his pride his hurt, nothing more.*

Chapter 13

Sasha stood at the desk of the police station and waited. She had only just moved to this town, and they didn't know her yet. They would soon figure out that she wasn't what they'd think right away. Sasha wasn't a crack pot, nor was she someone seeking fame. She'd had that once, and that hadn't gone over nearly as well as she thought it might have. Though why she ever tried was beyond her. People didn't like her.

Not that she cared. Sasha would either be able to help the police department or not. She would tell the people who came to her about it, and they'd take their anger out on them, not her. Rubbing the bruise on her butt, she wondered if Hailey would be at her home when she went back. Didn't these people want to solve murders?

"Miss?" She told the man her name. "Miss Harvard, the captain, he says that he didn't have time for crack balls."

"Tell him that's fine. I don't care one way or the other." She picked up her purse and snapped her gum at the young man. "I just do what they tell me, then I'm out of it."

"You can tell me. I have a friend, he's not a cop anymore, but he can maybe help you. Mr. Bishop, he worked for a larger precinct than this one, but he's a good guy." She asked him why he wasn't a cop anymore. "He got married. They're nice people. I really like his wife, Raven. She's a hoot." Sasha cleared her throat. "Yes, here, let me call him, and you can talk to him about what you told me."

The phone was answered by a male. Sasha, knowing nothing about Mr. Bishop, thought that it was him. She told him her name and who she'd been talking to. The man was silent on the other end, and Sasha figured out he wasn't the right man.

"I need to talk to Sawyer Bishop, please. I have some important news for him." He asked her to hold on and she waited by the desk. There were so many ghosts in this place she wondered if anyone had ever wondered why it was so flipping cold all the time. Someone took her off hold. "Hello?"

"Dad said to tell you he'd be right here. He's got some major messes going on. Cooking isn't his best effort." Sasha told her that she'd wait. "Okay. Do you work for the police department here in town?"

"No. I just got to town and someone told me that I should talk to your dad. He used to be a cop." The girl said that he worked security now, and was liking that better. "Yes, well, I think I would too if I had the time. Is he going to be much longer? I have to get out of here before someone knows what I can do."

"Hello?" Finally, Sasha thought. "My name is Sawyer Bishop. What can I do for you? If you're calling me to bail you out, I'm not in the market."

"No, I'm not...do women call you up often and ask you

to bail them out?" Sawyer told her that the caller ID for the phone she'd called from came from the local police, and that he didn't normally bail anyone out. "Good, I guess. Okay, you can believe me or not, but the woman, Hailey Riddle, she can be found at the bottom of the lake at the south side of town. From the looks of her, I'd say that she was tied to a couple of cinder blocks and dropped into the water a few days ago."

"I'm sorry." She smiled. At least he'd not hung up on her. Not yet, at any rate. "First of all, how do you know that she's in the lake, and secondly, are you telling me that you did it?"

"No. She said that her husband did it. Like I'd say that I did it—if I did—while standing in the middle of a police station. Moron. His mistress was getting jealous of all the time he was spending with her. Go figure. This is why I will never marry. But he tied her to the cinder blocks and dropped her in the night that she came home from the gym." Sawyer asked if Patterson had put her up to this. "I don't know anyone named Patterson, but this is the truth. They come to me, the dead, and have me find them. I don't help them with causes or other shit like that. Just finding them. Once they're found, they just disappear. I don't know where they go, nor do I care, but that's what I do."

"For a job." She said no, she did it for fun. It was a blast having people, dead people, wake her in the middle of the night to beg for help. "I'm sorry. I don't understand this. You're sort of snarky, aren't you?"

"No, whatever gave you that idea? Anyway, you can use it or not, I've done my part. So if you'll have a nice day, I'll be—"

"Wait. I need more information." She said she wasn't giving him any of her personal shit. "I wasn't going to ask you. I figured you had enough on your hands with the dead and all. I don't remember anyone saying anything about a missing wife. Nor do I know the name Riddle. Can you give me a little more, please?"

"Okay. Usually this is about where someone hangs up on me, after they call me all sorts of names. Crackpot is one of the top ones. People can be so imaginative when they're being insulting, don't you think?" He said that he wouldn't know. "I guess not. His name is Bradley Riddle. He works at Central Clothing. Mr. Riddle is currently living with his mistress, Ruby Rose. Just between the two of us, I don't think that's her real name."

The man laughed and Sasha smiled. It wasn't often that anyone would tolerate her sense of humor. "What can you tell me about Mrs. Riddle? Was she alive when put in the water? I mean, as I said, I know nothing other than her name you've given me."

"If she had any injuries, they're long gone now. She does have strangulation marks around her throat, but that's not what killed her. She said that he dropped her in alive, and that his last words to her were to enjoy the view. He's a sick fuck, if you ask me." He laughed again, and the young man that had given her this number pointed to the door. "I'm being asked to leave here. The captain, or whatever is the equivalent of a boss here, is not happy about my trying to get him to find this woman."

"All right. I'm going to ask you if you can meet me at the café on Maple. There are a lot of people there at this time of the day, and you won't have to worry about me hurting you." She said that she carried a gun. "Does that work with the dead too?"

"Usually. They sometimes forget that they're dead." She thought about the meeting. "Look buddy, I don't do things like this. I've been beaten to shit before when someone said *meet me some place, it's crowded, I won't hurt you.* I gave you all that I know."

"I'm sorry that there are pieces of shit out there. But I swear to you on the life of my unborn child that I will not harm you in any way." There might not be a child, her mind screamed at her. "I can even bring my daughter with me. She'll just be glad to meet someone else that's not really human."

"All right. But if you come too close to me, at any time, I will shoot you. What are you, anyway?" He told her what he was. "Of course. I hate cats. A great deal. You come too close and you'll be a dead one, got it?"

"I do. I swear. Molly and I will be there soon. She'll be the only kid without a cell phone in front of her face, much to her shame." She laughed again and hung up.

Sasha didn't like people all that much, living or dead. She hadn't had a good friend in longer than she could remember. And forget dating. It was difficult enough holding onto a relationship without the dead demanding your attention all the time. The one and only time she'd ever had sex had gotten her where she was today. A ghost helper.

Sitting at one of the outdoor tables, she understood what Sawyer had said. Everyone, babies included, had a device of some sort in front of their faces. One baby, still in a car seat, had one hanging above his little head while he was catching a nap while the thing blared on. Christ, she hated those things too. Devices, she told herself, not babies.

"Hi." She looked at the beautiful young girl. "Dad said that if you want an ice cream, he'll let me have one. Even if

188

you don't eat it, could you please get one too? I just got back with my GGMa from the cruise, and the ice cream was horrid. I know what you're thinking too—it's hard to mess up ice cream—but you'd be wrong. So, do you want one?"

"Yes. And I can tell you're related to your dad. You have the same sense of humor, don't you?" The girl brightened up as if she'd been holding a bulb and it turned on. Sasha had to smile with her. "You and your dad, you get ice cream here often?"

The man at the counter yelled for Molly, and she told him that she'd be right back. Watching the two of them together, she loved that they were so close. Sasha wasn't close to her family, and would never be again. which was fine by her. Molly yelled and asked her what ice cream she wanted, and Sawyer rolled his eyes and told her to go ask.

"I want chocolate," Sasha yelled back, and got the thumbs up from Molly. She could easily fall in love with this kid.

When they sat down, she looked at the monster ice cream that she'd been handed.

"I didn't want you to leave until we got to know each other. My wife, Raven, she said that I would scare people off by offering them food. But it's not gotten me killed so far." Sasha licked her cone. "Okay, do you see anyone around here? The reason I ask is, we have two missing teenagers. The department thinks that they've run away from home. I don't."

"How old?" She didn't look around too much, but just took a general glance around the area. "There are four here, both hanging out with one of the other. Something you should know; they can't talk to each other unless they died together."

"One is sixteen, the other seventeen. Not that it matters, but the girl is older. They'd be wearing, I think, prom clothing."

She nodded at him. "I hate that. I bet you do as well. How do I find out anything about them? I'm assuming that you don't want to draw attention to yourself."

"I don't. Not from the living, but the dead. They know what I am, just not much more than that. Like what I look like. I've never asked if I give off dead people vibes or not, but how the hell does one get lessons on this crap? Molly, you're not going to see them. Sorry, chicky." Molly nodded and went back to her ice cream. "I can talk to them here, but I can tell you something about them. I'd say car crash. He has a nasty wound on his head. The girl has her neck broken. They were neither wearing seat belts that I can tell."

"How do you know that part?" She told him. "Okay, no marks. I see marks on them when I see them, but I didn't know what you saw."

"I see them as they were in death. I don't get a pretty picture of them, just the whole thing. The boy, he has some water on his pant legs. The girl hasn't any shoes on nor a long dress, so I can't tell. Perhaps a body of water." He was writing things down while she spoke. Molly would ask a question or two, but nothing more than that. "Hold on, Sawyer, they figured out that I can help them."

Not only did she get their names, Paul and Jenny, but she was able to tell Sawyer where their car was. Paul told her that he thought that someone had hit them in the rear, but he didn't know for sure. Then they just disappeared. Getting help was all she was able to do for them.

"Can I pay you for this? There is a reward for finding them." Sasha said she was good. "I'm sorry that you have to go through all this. But I do appreciate the help. Their parents still hold out hope that they're alive. This will be hard on them, but they will have closure."

After he left her, leaving his phone number for her if she needed anything else, Sasha sat there for a time and ate her ice cream. No one bothered her, for which she was grateful. She just enjoyed the day, and didn't think about anything but the chocolate cone that was bigger than her head.

~*~

Chandler was going back to college in January. He was also taking some classes online. He'd already taken a couple of them over the last few weeks and passed them, but now he was ready to dig his teeth into the real stuff.

"You ready for it?" Chandler told his mom that he was as ready as he'd ever be. "I know you'll do just fine, Chandler. You're a bright man."

Chandler thanked her. "I don't have to take the entire load. I get credit for doing the work around here, like birthing the animals and working with Doctor Joe when he needs it. They said that he thought I'd do a good job too. And he said that I can work for him while I'm going to school. That'll help."

"I bet it will." Mom sat with him. "Did you know that Raven paid off all our bills for your dad and I? I'm telling you that so that if you need help with books and stuff, we can set some money aside for you if you need it."

"Sawyer is helping me out with that too. He's even giving me his old car so that I can have something to drive back and forth to class. I couldn't have done this without their help." Mom didn't move, so he knew that she had something else on her mind. "I even was able to afford some new clothing, thanks to Raven and her letting me go through some of the things she has for sale. I think the rest of my brothers did it as well."

"You aren't going to leave me, are you, Chandler?" He asked her what she meant. "I don't think I want to think about the day when you boys leave home. I know that Sawyer is only about twenty minutes away, but he doesn't live here. If another one of you leave me, I don't know what I'll do."

"Mom, you will always have us around for you, whatever you need." She said that she knew, but she was feeling low because her boys, she called them, were leaving the nest. "Mom, we should have been kicked from the nest a long time ago. The only way that I'd leave here is when I find me a mate. And I don't foresee that happening, do you?"

"I hope you find someone to love you. The greatest joy in the world is having someone share your life with you. Why, while there are times I want to brain your father, I don't want him to leave me. I'd die, I think." He told her not to talk like that. "Honey, it's going to happen someday. Sooner for me, because I'm older than you, but we all die."

Chandler kissed her hand and told her that he loved her. "You're the best woman I've ever met, Mom. If you leave me, in any way, I don't know what I'll do with myself."

"You'll be just fine." She started to stand up and looked back at him. "Did you hear that they found Paul and Jenny? Poor kids. Both of them dead. Sawyer told me that he thinks they were hit from behind. There were tire marks, he said, but not from the driver that hit them. Their poor mothers must be dying about now."

Mom started a pot of water for iced tea. Chandler told her what he knew, which wasn't much. Just that they'd been almost in the water, and that would have made it impossible for them to have been found.

"Sawyer said that they weren't driving fast, it looks like to him, but they're going to do a lot of investigations before they let this go." He thought of something else that his brother had told him. "Sawyer seems to think that the police should have done a better job of looking for them instead of thinking that they just ran off. Perhaps they could have saved them, you think?"

"I don't know. Horrible business, being a cop." He agreed with her. "Are you staying for dinner tonight? We're having burgers and brats. I just love that new grill we got. Just go out and turn it on. No more waiting on the charcoal to heat up enough. Your dad acts like he invented the thing, he's having so much fun with it. Oh, and to think that next year we'll have a little baby to have fun out there with. Your father is already looking at plans to get a swing set for the little one. I'm so glad that they didn't wait to tell us about the baby until later. I'm so excited about being a grandma again. With little Molly, we'll have two."

They'd told them about the baby last Sunday, as it was getting difficult for them to keep the secret. Chandler didn't think that would be anything he'd be able to keep to himself either.

"I heard that you were having a grill out every night." She said that they were. "Good for you guys. Next year I'll see about getting you a nice picnic table so we can eat out there. We still have all that wood from when Dad built that shed out back."

"Oh, I'd love that. And with the new baby coming next year, I'll just be out there every day. I'm going to show her or him how to make jam too." Mom put the tea bags in and turned on her timer before sitting down again. "I did something silly.

I asked Sawyer if he would allow me to watch the baby. I thought they'd have nannies or something. They are, but they want us to have the baby whenever we want. Even if we had to take him or her from the nanny. Raven called me a few minutes later to tell me that I was going to be her helper in this. It's been a long time since she had a baby in the house, and she's worried too much has changed."

"I bet you've started reading up on it, haven't you? About the changes a baby will need." Mom laughed and said that she had a stack of books to read now. "Mom, you raised us up pretty well without books. I'm sure that you'll do just fine."

After hugging his mom again, he went out to the yard. He really wanted to get him a place of his own, but he thought that after talking to Mom, he'd wait a bit longer. With Sawyer not living at home anymore, there was certainly more hot water than there had been before.

Quincy pulled into the drive just as Chandler thought about going into town. "I was hoping that someone would be here. Want to go for a long run? I sure need it after signing up for classes today. Christ, I had no idea there would be so many to choose from." Chandler said he'd done that yesterday. "Do you believe this? We're able to go back to college and get a degree in what we wanted. I'm going to think of a way to pay back Raven and Sawyer. They turned the tide for us, I think."

They stripped down and took off running after shifting. Chandler hadn't been on a hard run in a while, and it felt good.

There were a good three or four miles from the house when he heard someone crying. Sneaking up behind the sound and where it was coming from, he was startled to see a baby lying next to a woman. Even from where he was, Chandler could tell that the woman was dead.

Sawyer, I have an issue here. He asked him if it could wait. *Nope. I found a body by the fence that divides the Little land from the Marks land. There's a newborn here too, and she's freezing. I'm taking her back to Mom.*

Okay, but don't touch anything else. I'll come by the house before I have you take me out to where she is. He said that he could do that, and gently picked the baby up in his mouth. *Chandler, just be careful. If she was murdered, then he might come back to take care of the baby too.*

I have Quincy with me. We'll meet you back at the house. Quincy asked if he should shift so as not to hurt the baby. *I thought of that. But it'll be slower moving. And she's very cold now. I'll contact Mom and have her get something warm to wrap her in.*

Chandler got back to the house in a few minutes. The baby was crying, but it was weak and he could feel her getting colder with each passing minute. Mom took her from him and wrapped her up in a blanket.

"I asked Sawyer if I should bathe her, to warm her up in some water, and he said to go ahead. He's afraid that whoever did this to her momma will come back for her." Mom was cooing at the child. "I have a bottle up there in the cabinet, Chandler. After you shift and dress, come back in here and help me out with her, won't you? Wesley, go out and milk old Margaret. The fresh milk will be good for her, I think."

After they finished getting what Mom wanted, they watched the little girl while she fed from the bottle. She was so tiny, Chandler realized that he could almost hold her in one hand. When the police showed up, he met them at the door and led them to the kitchen where Mom was. All they did was look at her and asked where the body was. That sort of pissed him off, but he held his temper.

Sawyer arrived a little while later. He had a woman with him, but they were following Quincy out to the fence line before he could meet her. She was a tiny thing too.

Molly came rushing in the house just as Mom was burping the baby. "She's beautiful, isn't she, Grandma?" Mom told Molly that she was, but tiny. "I wonder if I was that little. Mom said that I was over nine pounds. Is she that small?"

"No, honey. I think she's closer to only being about six or seven pounds. I asked Sawyer about it, and he said that your mom was bringing us some diapers and such for her. We'll get her all cleaned up, and then we'll dress her when your mom gets here."

Chandler noticed that the baby still had her umbilical cord intact, and she was a good color now that she'd had some dinner. There was a small birthmark on her foot, but other than that, she seemed perfect. Helping Mom give her a sponge bath—she told him babies couldn't have a real bath until the umbilical cord fell off—he had a moment or two of fright when he nearly let her slip from his hands. She was slippery, as well as so small.

It took them about an hour to make sure that she was going to be all right. Molly started calling her Pip for some reason, and that started them all calling her that. He was beginning to worry about his brother and the woman. They'd been gone a long time, he thought.

Mom asked him to rock Pip because she needed to get dinner started. The fried potatoes smelled heavenly, and he found himself talking to Pip about what he was going to have for dinner. When she opened her eyes and looked at him, Chandler had a feeling that she could understand every word that he said.

"I'm being silly." She just stared at him. "My brother should have come here to take care of you. He is the one that will be taking care of little people like you. Of course, I don't think it's much different than helping a pig come into the world. I didn't mean to make it sound like I was calling you a pig, but just that they're little and slippery too."

Rocking her in his arms, he wondered if this was what it felt like to have a child of your own. When Sawyer came back, he had more information on Pip's mother, but the woman, whoever she had been, had left.

Perhaps he'd look her up. She might be lonely, he told himself after Sawyer told them that she'd just moved to town. Chandler would have to beat his brothers to asking her out or he'd never get the chance. Not many women came to town that were unmarried anymore. And he'd like to go out on a date again. It had been a long time, he thought.

Chandler was excited about the new turns in his life. He just hoped that he did well in college. He wanted that more than anything right now.

Before You Go...

HELP AN AUTHOR

write a review

THANK YOU!

Share your voice and help guide other readers to these wonderful books. Even if it's only a line or two your reviews help readers discover the author's books so they can continue creating stories that you'll love. Login to your favorite retailer and leave a review. Thank you.

AWARD WINNING, BESTSELLING AUTHOR

Kathi Barton, winner of the Pinnacle Book Achievement award as well as a best-selling author on Amazon and All Romance books, lives in Nashport, Ohio with her husband Paul. When not creating new worlds and romance, Kathi and her husband enjoy camping and going to auctions. She can also be seen at county fairs with her husband who is an artist and potter.

Her muse, a cross between Jimmy Stewart and Hugh Jackman, brings her stories to life for her readers in a way that has them coming back time and again for more. Her favorite genre is paranormal romance with a great deal of spice. You can visit Kathi online and drop her an email if you'd like. She loves hearing from her fans. aaronskiss@gmail.com.

Follow Kathi on her blog: http://kathisbartonauthor.blogspot.com/